Praise for the *New York Times* bestselling series

An *ambitious intern.*
A perfectionist executive.
And a whole lot of name calling.

"Filled with plenty of hot sex and sizzling tens.

—RT Book Reviews

". . . deliciously steamy . . ."

—*EW.com*

"A devilishly depraved cross between a hardcore porn and a very special episode of *The Office.* . . . For us fetish-friendly fiends to feast on!!"

–PerezHilton.com

"Smart, sexy, and satisfying, Christina Lauren's *Beautiful Bastard* is destined to become a romance classic."

—Tara Sue Me, bestselling
author of *The Submissive*

"The perfect blend of sex, sass and heart, *Beautiful Bastard* is a steamy battle of wills that will get your blood pumping!"

—S. C. Stephens, *New York Times*
bestselling author of *Thoughtless*

"*Beautiful Bastard* has heart, heat, and a healthy dose of snark. Romance readers who love a smart plot are in for an amazingly sexy treat!"

—**Myra McEntire, author of** *Hourglass*

"*Beautiful Bastard* is the perfect mix of passionate romance and naughty eroticism. I couldn't, and didn't, put it down until I'd read every last word."

—**Elena Raines,** *Twilightish*

Beautiful STRANGER

A charming British playboy.
A girl determined to finally live.
And a secret liaison revealed in all too vivid color.

"*Hot* . . . if you like your hook-ups early and plentiful . . ."

—**EW.com**

"The thing that I love the most about Christina Lauren and the duo's *Beautiful* books is that there is always humor in them. As well as hot steamy moments and some of the sweetest I love you's."

—**BooksSheReads.com**

Beautiful BITCH

CHRISTINA LAUREN

G

GALLERY BOOKS

NEW YORK • LONDON • TORONTO • SYDNEY • NEW DELHI

G

Gallery Books
A Division of Simon & Schuster, Inc.
1230 Avenue of the Americas
New York, NY 10020

First Gallery Books trade paperback edition July 2013

GALLERY BOOKS and colophon are registered trademarks of
Simon & Schuster, Inc.

For information about special discounts for bulk purchases, please
contact Simon & Schuster Special Sales at 1-866-506-1949 or
business@simonandschuster.com.

The Simon & Schuster Speakers Bureau can bring authors to your
live event. For more information or to book an event, contact the
Simon & Schuster Speakers Bureau at 1-866-248-3049 or visit our
website at www.simonspeakers.com.

Manufactured in the United States of America

10 9 8 7 6 5 4

Library of Congress Cataloging-in-Publication Data
Lauren, Christina.
    Beautiful bitch / Christina Lauren. -- First Gallery Books Trade paperback
edition.
    pages cm
    I. Title.
    PS3612.A9442273B45 2013
    813'.6--dc23

                                                                2013019309

ISBN 978-1-4767-5414-7
ISBN 978-1-4767-5172-6 (ebook)

To the readers who wanted more, this one is for you.

Yes, you.

ONE

My mother always told me to find a woman who would be my equal in every way.

"Don't let yourself fall for someone who'll put your world before theirs. Fall for the powerhouse who lives as fearlessly as you do. Find the woman who makes you want to be a better man."

I'd definitely found my equal, the woman who made my life a living hell and lived to antagonize me. A woman whose mouth I wanted to tape shut . . . every bit as much as I wanted to kiss it.

My girlfriend, my former intern, Miss Chloe Mills. *Beautiful Bitch.*

At least, that's how I used to see her, back when I was an idiot and blind to how hopelessly in love I was with her. I'd most certainly found the woman who made me want to be a better man; I had fallen for the fearless one. It just so happened that most days I was unable to get more than two minutes alone with her.

My life: finally get the girl, never actually get to see her.

———

I'd been traveling for the better part of the last two months in search of office space for the Ryan Media Group branch we were setting up in New York. Chloe stayed behind, and while our recent—and rare—weekend together here in Chicago was full of friends, sunshine, and leisure, the time alone with her wasn't nearly enough. We'd socialized the entire weekend, from morning until well past midnight, stumbling back to my place each night, and would barely manage to get our clothes off before having quiet, sleepy sex.

The truth was, our lovemaking each night—which had grown both more intimate and more wild over time, and allowed us only minimal sleep—still never felt like enough. I kept waiting for it to feel like we were settled, or had established some solid routine. But it never happened. I was in a constant state of longing. And Mondays were the worst. Mondays we had wall-to-wall meetings, and the entire workweek stretched out ahead of me: bleak and Chloeless.

Hearing the familiar cadence of heels clicking on the tile, I looked up from where I stood at the printer waiting for some documents to appear. As if hearing my inner plea, Chloe Mills walked toward me, wearing a slim red wool skirt, a fitted navy sweater, and heels that, quite frankly, didn't look very safe outside of the bedroom. When I'd left early this morning to prepare for an eight o'clock meeting, the only thing she'd been wearing was a pale beam of light from the sunrise through the bedroom window.

I suppressed my smile, and tried not to look too desperate, but I don't know why I bothered. She could read my every expression.

"I see you've found the magic machine that takes whatever is on your computer screen and puts it on paper," she called. "In *ink*."

I slid my hand into my pants pocket, jiggled some change there, and felt a trickle of adrenaline slip into my veins at her teasing tone and approach. "Actually, I discovered this wonderful contraption my first day here. I just liked the moments of blissful quiet when I'd make you get up and leave the outer office to retrieve my documents."

She stalked toward me, her smile wide and eyes mischievous. "Asshole."

Fuck, yes. Come to me, lovely. Ten minutes in the copy room? I could easily make your day in those ten minutes.

"You're in for a workout tonight," she whispered as, without slowing her pace, she patted my shoulder and continued past me down the hall.

I stared at her ass as she gave it a little shake, and waited for her to come back and torture me some more. She didn't. *That's it? That's all I get? A pat on the shoulder, some verbal foreplay, and an ass-wiggle?*

Still, tonight: our first full evening alone together in weeks.

We'd been in love for over a year—and fucking longer

than that—and we'd yet to have more than the length of a weekend alone together since San Diego.

I sighed and pulled my papers from the printer tray. We needed a vacation.

———

Back in my office, I dropped the files on my desk and stared at my computer monitor, which, to my surprise, displayed a mostly empty calendar. I'd pulled insanely long workdays the entire week before just so I could get home to Chloe early, so aside from Payroll grabbing me early this morning, my schedule had remained open. Chloe, however, was clearly busy in her new position.

I missed having her as my intern. I missed bossing her around. I *really* missed her bossing me around in return.

For the first time in months, I had time to sit in my office and literally do nothing. I closed my eyes and a hundred thoughts filtered past in mere seconds: the view of the empty New York offices just before I'd left for the airport. The prospect of packing up my house. The far preferable prospect of unpacking in a new home with Chloe. And then my brain went down its favorite path: Chloe naked and in every conceivable position.

Which led back to one of my favorite memories of Chloe and me: the morning after her presentation. Due to the heat and tension that came with actually admitting we were no longer hate-fucking but actually interested in something more, we had had one of our biggest arguments ever. I hadn't seen her in months, so I showed up at her presentation for the scholarship board to watch her nail it. And she did.

Afterward, though, despite everything we'd said upstairs in the boardroom, there was still so much *more* to say. The reality of our reunion still felt so new, and I hadn't been sure where we stood.

———

Once we were on the sidewalk, I stared down at her: at her eyes, and lips, and her neck, which was still a little red from the biting kisses I'd placed there only minutes before. The way she reached up and rubbed her finger over what appeared to be a small hickey pushed an electric reminder from my brain to my cock: this reunion is nice but it's time to get her home and fuck her into the mattress.

I wasn't sure we were on the same page about that, though.

Outside in the daylight, she looked like she was about to fall over. Of course she was. Knowing Chloe, she'd probably been preparing and fine-tuning her presentation for the last seventy-two hours straight, no sleep. But I hadn't seen her in so long—could I keep it together long enough to just let her go home to rest? If she needed to nap, I could just hang out and wait for her to wake up, right? I could lie down near her, reassure myself that she was really here and we were really doing this and just . . . what? Touch her hair?

5

Holy shit. Had I always been this creepy?

Chloe hitched her computer bag up over her shoulder, and the movement pulled me out of my thoughts. But when I blinked back into focus, I saw that she was staring off into the distance, toward the river.

"You okay?" I asked, ducking to meet her eyes.

She nodded, startling a little as if she'd been caught. "I'm fine, just overwhelmed."

"A little shell-shocked?"

Her exhausted smile pulled at something tender beneath my ribs, but the way she licked her lips before speaking tugged inside me a bit lower. "I was so sad thinking I wasn't going to see you today. And this morning, I spent the entire walk between your building and here thinking how weird it was that I was going to be doing this without you, or Elliott, or anyone from Ryan Media. And then you came here, and of course you pissed me off, but you also made me laugh . . ." She tilted her head, studied my face. "The presentation was exactly what I wanted it to be, and then the job offers . . . and you. You told me you love me. You're here."

She reached out to press her palm flat to my chest. I knew she could feel my heart slamming against my sternum. "My adrenaline is slowing and now I'm just . . ." She moved her hand away from me and waved it in front of her before it seemed to deflate at her side. "I'm not sure how tonight is going to work."

How tonight was going to work? I could tell her exactly how it would work. We'd talk until it was dark, and then fuck until the sun came up. I reached for her, slipping my arm around her shoulder. Christ, she felt good.

"Let me worry about all of that. I'll drive you home."

This time she shook her head, pulling more fully back into the moment. "It's okay if you have to go back to work, we can—"

Scowling, I growled, "Don't be ridiculous. It's almost four. I'm not going back to work. My car is here and you're getting in it."

Her smile turned sharp at the corners. "Bossy Bennett emerges. Now I'm definitely not going with you."

"Chloe, I'm not kidding. I'm not letting you out of my sight until Christmas."

She squinted up at the late afternoon June sun. "Christmas? That sounds a little gimp-in-the-basement for my tastes."

"If you're not into that, this relationship might not work after all," I teased.

She laughed, but didn't answer. Instead, those deep brown eyes stared up at me, unblinking and hard to read.

I felt so out of practice with this, and struggled to hide my frustration.

Placing my hands on her hips, I bent to press a small kiss to the center of her mouth. Fuck, I needed more. "Let's go. No basements. Just us."

"Bennett—"

I cut her off with another kiss, paradoxically relaxed by this tiny disagreement. "My car. Now."

"You sure you don't want to hear what I have to say?"

"Absolutely positive. You can talk all you want once I have my face firmly planted between your legs."

Chloe nodded and followed when I took her hand and gently pulled her toward the parking deck, but she was smiling mysteriously all the while.

———

The entire drive to her place, she tickled her fingers up and down my thigh, leaned to lick my neck, slid her hand over my cock, and talked about the tiny red panties she put on this morning, needing that little confidence boost.

"Will it shatter your confidence if I tear them off?" I asked, leaning to kiss her at a red light. The car behind me honked just when it was getting good: when her lips were giving way to tiny bites and her sounds filled my mouth and my head and—fuck—my entire chest. I needed to get her naked and beneath me.

In the elevator on the way up to her apartment, it was wild. She was here, holy fuck she was here, and I'd missed her so much; if I had my way, this night was going to last for three days. She pushed her skirt up over her hips, and I lifted her, stepping between her legs and pressing my aching cock into her.

"Going to make you come so many times," I promised.

"Mmm, promise?"

"Promise."

I rocked my hips against her and she gasped, whispering, "Okay, but first—"

The elevator dinged and she wiggled herself free, slipping to the floor. With a hesitating look, Chloe smoothed her skirt back down, and walked ahead of me into the hallway and toward her apartment.

My stomach dropped.

I hadn't been back here since we were apart and I'd conned her security guard into letting me up to talk to her. I'd ended up spending the entire time conversing with the outside of her door instead. I felt strangely anxious. I wanted to only feel relieved at our reunion, not think about everything we'd missed out on in our months apart. To distract myself, I bent low and sucked at the skin beneath her ear and began working on the zipper at the back of her skirt as she fumbled with her key.

She swung the door open, turning to me. "Bennett—" she started, but I pushed her inside and back against the nearest wall, quieting her with my mouth. Fuck, she tasted good, a mix of the lemon water she'd been drinking and that familiar taste she always had: soft mint and softer, hungry lips. My fingers teased at the back of her skirt but I lost my finesse, yanking the zipper down and shoving the fabric to the floor, *immediately reaching for her blazer.* Why the fuck is she still wearing this goddamn thing? Why is she still wearing anything?

Beneath her deep purple dress shirt, her nipples hardened as I stared, and I reached out to circle one with a fingertip. Her sharp gasp pulled my eyes to hers.

"I missed this. I missed you."

Her tongue peeked out to wet her lips. "Me, too."

"Fuck, I love you."

When I kissed her throat, her chest lifted and fell with quickened breaths, and I wasn't sure how this was going to go down, how I could possibly slow down. Would I take her here, fast and hard first, or would I carry her to a couch or chair, kneel down, and just taste her? I'd been thinking about all of it for so long—playing out in my head how every scenario would go—and in the moment I felt a little paralyzed by the reality of her here, in the flesh.

I needed it all. I needed to feel her sounds and her skin, lose myself in the comfort of her hand wrapped around me, watch the sweat bead her brow while she rode me, showing me how much she'd missed me, too. I'd see it in the way her rhythm would falter when she got closer, or she would clutch me when I would say her name in that quiet whisper she always liked.

My hands shook as I reached up and carefully slipped her top button free. It registered somewhere in the evershrinking evolved portion of my brain that I didn't want to destroy the buttons on the shirt she'd worn for her thesis defense.

I also wanted to savor this. Savor her.

"Bennett?"

"Mmm?" I undid another button, ran a finger across the hollow of her throat.

"I love you," she said, her hands braced on my forearms, eyes wide. My hands faltered, and I lost my breath. "But . . . you're going to hate what I'm about to tell you."

I was still stuck on the I love you. My grin felt a little out of control. "What . . . ? Whatever you have to say, I'm sure I won't hate it."

She winced, turning to look at the clock on the wall. It was the first time it occurred to me to take a look around her apartment. I stepped back in surprise; her place looked nothing like I expected.

Everything about Chloe had always been impeccable, stylish, current. But her apartment could not be farther from that description. The living room was tidy, but full of worn furniture and things that didn't look like anything she would own. Everything was brown and tan; the couches looked comfortable but like they were made out of the same material as a stuffed animal. A small collection of wooden owls was clustered on a shelf near a tiny television and, in the kitchen, the clock that she'd glanced at had a big smiling bumblebee on the face with the words "Bee Happy!" in garish bubble letters.

"This . . . is not what I expected."

Chloe followed my attention around the apartment and then let a loud laugh burst free. It was the same laugh she used to let out before she would verbally eviscerate me. "What would you have expected, Mr. Ryan?"

I shrugged, not wanting to insult her but feeling sincerely curious about this disconnect. "I just expected your place to look a little more like you."

"What, you don't like my owls?" she asked, grinning.

"I do, yes, they just—" I started, running a nervous hand into my hair.

"And these couches?" she interrupted. "Don't you think we could have fun on them?"

"Baby, we could have fun on any surface in this place, I'm just saying I expected your place to be less . . ."

Fuck. Why was I still talking? I looked over at her and she had a hand over her mouth, laughing silently.

"Calm down," she said. "This was my mom's apartment. I love it, but you're right. None of this stuff is mine. When I was in school it just didn't make sense for me to sell it, or to get new things."

I took another curious glance around. "You could buy yourself hundred-dollar panties but you didn't want a new couch?"

"Don't be such a snob. I didn't need a new couch. And I frequently needed new panties," she said quietly, meaningfully.

"Hell yes you did."

With this perfect reminder, I stepped close to her, resuming my gentle attack on her line of buttons. Pushing her shirt over her shoulders and down her arms, I stared at where she stood in front of me, in only a red lace bra and matching underwear. They were tiny.

"Tell me what you want," I said, feeling a little desperate as I pushed her hair behind her shoulder so I could suck on her neck, her jaw, her ear. "My cock? My mouth? My hands? Christ, I'm doing it all tonight but where does one start? I haven't seen you in months and feel like I'm losing my mind."

I reached for her arm, urging her closer. "Baby, put your hands on me."

She ran her hands up my neck and cupped my face. I could feel her shaking. "Bennett."

Only when she said my name like this—like she was shy and maybe even anxious—did I remember she said she had something to tell me other than I love you. Something I wouldn't like.

"What is it?"

Her eyes were enormous, searching mine and full of apology. "I just finished my defense, and—"

"Oh, shit. I'm such an ass. I should take you to dinner or—"

"—and I promised Julia and Sara that we would go out—"

"—maybe we could get some dinner after I make you come—" I barreled on.

"—for drinks after my presentation—"

"I just need to hear you come once and then we can go. Just give me . . ." I stopped, finally letting her words settle in. "Wait, what? You're going out with Julia and Sara? Tonight?"

She nodded, eyes tight. "I didn't know you'd be here. I can't tell you how much I want to call and cancel. But the thing is, I can't. Not after how good they've been to me the last few months . . . when you and I were . . ."

I groaned, pressing the heel of my hands to my eyes. "Why didn't you tell me this before I got you naked? Holy shit, how am I supposed to let you go now? I'm going to be hard for hours."

"I tried to tell you." To her credit, she looked as frustrated as I felt.

"Do we have time to . . ." I shook my head, looking around as if the answer were buried somewhere in this ancient furniture. "I could probably get us both off in, like, two minutes."

She laughed. "I'm not sure that's something to brag about."

The hell it wasn't.

Her small gasp of surprise was stolen by my lips as I kissed her, tongue and teeth and not even caring if we only had a few minutes. I could do a few minutes.

I slid my hand over the racing pulse in her throat, between her breasts and lower, down the front of her stomach. I moved lower still, finding that familiar, favorite place where she was warm and slick, and the roof could fall in and I wouldn't even notice because, God, nothing existed but her and her little sounds and quiet whispers to keep going, keep going.

"Bennett," she whispered. "Please."

I reached down for my own pants, and had just started to speak—

And was interrupted by a sharp knock on the door.

A familiar voice floated into her entryway. "We're here, Miss Serious Business Graduate, and we're ready for the drinking!"

"This is a joke. Tell me this is a joke," *I said, glaring at her.*

She shook her head, biting back a smile.

"I am in no mood to share right now. You have got to be fucking *kidding me.*"

"I forget how much I love seeing you on an angry tear."

She walked to the door in her fucking underwear, and opened it a crack before turning and sprinting into her bedroom, leaving me to greet the intruders.

What in the actual fuck.

"I'll be out in a few!" *Chloe yelled over her shoulder, her nearly bare ass disappearing into a bedroom down the hall.*

Julia whistled loudly, stepping over the threshold, and then stopped, and broke into laughter when she saw me.

"Wow, I didn't expect you to answer the door in your underwear, Chloe." *Sara walked in with her hands over her eyes, reaching out blindly. She grabbed a handful of my half-unbuttoned shirt and shrieked when she uncovered her eyes and saw that it was me she was holding on to.* "Mr. Ryan!"

"Hello, ladies," *I said, voice flat. I straightened my shirt, pulled my tie back into place.*

"Oh boy, did we interrupt something?" Julia asked, eyes wide and teasing.

"Yes, in fact. We were . . . becoming reacquainted."

Chloe called out from one of the bedrooms down the hall to help ourselves to the champagne in the fridge, and I tried to ignore the way Julia's eyes dropped to my zipper. I stood still, letting her take a good long look. My erection was gone anyway.

Mostly.

"I didn't realize it was to be a girls' night out," I said, when the silence felt like it had dragged on forever.

Sara stepped back, her eyes seeming to struggle to stay above my shoulders, and explained, "I don't think any of us expected you to be here and . . . want a night in."

I most definitely wanted a night in. In every part of Chloe.

Julia studied me for a minute and then smiled. "I'll admit I was pretty sure Bennett would be here."

I couldn't help but mirror her grin. She had, after all, called me to urge me to go to Chloe's presentation. She was obviously on my side.

Even if she had interrupted my attempt to fuck Chloe for the first time in forever.

I turned, moving into the kitchen to wash my hands. Julia followed, and behind me I heard her open the bottle of champagne, the squeak and pop and then the quiet fizz reminding me how much I'd rather be opening that bottle over Chloe's naked body, and licking the foamy bubbles from her skin.

Julia continued, "But I think we should all go out to celebrate, and he can have as much of her as he wants." She poured four flutes of champagne and then handed one to me. "You'll just have to wait until later to . . . reacquaint."

Chloe emerged from her room in black skinny jeans, strappy black heels, and a shimmering blue tank top that made her skin look golden.

No way in hell would I be able to keep my hands off her if she wore that out.

"Chloe," I started, walking over to her and setting my champagne down on the kitchen counter with a shaking hand. I scowled at her hair, tied back in a sleek low ponytail.

Her eyes sparkled with amusement and she stretched to reach my ear so only I could hear. "You can take it down later."

"You should count on it."

"Do you want to grab it? Pull it?" she asked, kissing the shell of my ear. I nodded, eyes closing. "Or do you want to feel my hair down and loose on your stomach while my mouth works your cock?"

I reached for my champagne with a shaky hand, downed it. "Let's go with yes."

Need coiled low in my stomach and I was torn between wanting to smash something and wanting to drag her back into her bedroom and peel those jeans down her legs. Absolutely no part of me felt like spending an evening drinking wine and eating cheese and listening to girl talk. I wasn't sure I'd be able to keep it together.

As if reading my mind, she whispered, "It'll just make it better when we get home."

"I doubt that is even possible."

Her fingers lightly scratched over my chest. "I've missed that surly face."

Ignoring her, I asked, "How about you come to my place later? Go out with the girls, enjoy this night. I'll be there when you're ready."

She stretched and slid a slow, warm kiss across my mouth. "What happened to not letting me out of your sight until Christmas?"

———

I'd expected a dance club, maybe something fancy with twenty-dollar drinks and miles of twenty-something coeds in tiny black dresses. What I hadn't expected was a low-key bar in the suburbs, with darts and what Julia called "the best sampling of beer in Illinois."

As long as they could make me a vodka gimlet and I could be in constant physical contact with Chloe, the night might not be too much of a disaster. I followed the girls inside, shooting daggers at every leering douchebag in the place as we made our way up to the bar. Julia plopped herself down on a worn leather stool, shouting something to the bartender about the usual for the ladies and something pink for the pretty boy.

On second thought, this was going to be a long night.

Sara—clearly still a bit unnerved by my company—sat on the other side of Chloe, and made her recount every last detail about her defense. Chloe told her about Clarence Cheng, about how I'd barged in there and been an asshole, how she'd presented both projects, and even been offered a job.

"Two jobs," I clarified, staring her down so she knew I was thinking she'd better damn well fucking take the job at RMG.

She rolled her eyes but none of us could miss her proud smile. With their beers and my pink Cosmo raised in the air, we toasted Chloe on a job well done.

Beside me she downed her beer and then wiggled off her seat. "Who's up for some darts?"

Sara raised her hand and jumped a little. After a single beer, she seemed tipsy and loose enough to not act like we were still in the office. I slid my gaze down the length of Chloe's body. I rather liked the idea of watching her stretching and moving to play darts in that tight little number.

"You coming?" she asked, leaning down and pressing her breasts into my forearm.

Fucking tease.

"Hoping to, very soon." I let my eyes linger on her mouth before dropping to her chest. Beneath the thin fabric of her top, her nipples pebbled.

Her laugh brought my attention back to her red lips and she pushed them together in a playful pout. "Is Bennett a little keyed up?"

"Bennett is a lot keyed up," I said, pulling her between my legs and kissing the curve of her ear. I wanted to be patient and let her enjoy this night, but patience had never really been my strong suit. "Bennett wants Chloe naked and touching his cock."

With a giggle, she danced away and to the back of the bar, her arm linked with Sara's.

Julia put her hand on my shoulder, glancing quickly behind us to make sure Chloe was out of earshot. "You did good."

I was uncomfortable discussing personal issues with all but a few people in my life, and this most personal of all conversations was the last thing I wanted to have with a virtual stranger. Still, Julia had taken the time to track me down for Chloe's sake. That definitely took balls.

"Thank you for the call," I said. "But I do want you to know I would have gone to her anyway. I couldn't stay away anymore."

Julia took a sip of her beer. "I figured if you were anything like her, you were about to head in for another round. I called because I wanted you to have that confidence you needed to go in and just be your best bastard self."

"I wasn't too much of a bastard." I frowned, considering. "I don't think."

"I'm sure," Julia drawled. "You're the portrait of compromise."

Ignoring this, I lifted my fruity girl drink and drained it.

"She's so happy tonight," Julia murmured, almost to herself.

"She's thin." I glanced at where she stood, poised and ready to throw a dart. She did seem happy, and for that I was thrilled, but the difference in her body was also hard for me to ignore. "Too thin."

Nodding, Julia said, "She exercised too much, worked too much." Her eyes searched mine for a beat before she added, "It wasn't good, Bennett. She was a wreck."

"So was I."

She acknowledged this with a teasing smile. The sadness was in the past, after all. "So if you're going to keep her in bed for the next few days, just make sure you give her breaks to eat."

I nodded, moving my eyes to the back of the room, where my girl spun a couple of times, took aim, and then barely hit the dartboard. She and Sara broke into laughter, pausing only to say something that then made them both laugh harder.

And while she played and danced to the Rolling Stones, I felt the weight of my love for her settle into a heavy warmth in my stomach. Two months apart was nothing in the grand scheme of what we had ahead of us, but in our shared history it felt enormous. I wanted to dwarf it with time spent together.

I needed to get back, get closer. I waved to the bartender, mouthing, "Check," when she looked at me.

Julia stopped me with a warning hand on my arm. "Don't fuck it up. She's independent, and she's been doing it on her own for so long she'll never be the girl to tell you how much she needs you. But she'll show you how much she wants this. Chloe is about action, not words. I've known her since we were twelve, and you're it for her."

Two smooth arms slipped around my waist from behind, and Chloe pressed a kiss between my shoulder blades. "What are we talking about over here?"

"Football," Julia said just as I answered, "Politics."

I felt her laugh and she slid under my arm, wrapping herself around me. "So you were talking about me."

"Yes," we both answered.

"And what a mess I was and how happy I look tonight, and how Bennett better not fuck it up this time."

Julie glanced at me, punting that one in my direction as she lifted her beer, raised it in a silent toast, and then left us alone at the end of the bar.

Chloe turned her brown eyes on me. "Did she tell you all of my secrets?"

"Hardly." I set my drink down and wrapped my arm around her. "Can we go now? I've been away from you for too long and I'm reaching the limit on how much sharing I'm willing to tolerate. I want you alone."

I felt her laugh as a small shaking of her body in my arm, and then the quiet sound made it to my ears. "You're so demanding."

"I'm just telling you what I want."

"Fine then. Be specific. What do you really want?"

"I want you on your knees on my bed. I want you sweaty and begging. I want you wet enough to drink from."

"Shit," she whispered, her voice strung tight. "I'm already there."

"Then damn, Miss Mills. Get the fuck in my car."

Two

With my hands on the steering wheel, and her hands everywhere else—my thighs, my cock, my neck, my chest—I wasn't even sure we would make it home safely.

Especially not once she lifted my right arm so she could duck down and unzip my pants, pull my cock from my boxers, and drag her tongue up its length. I'd wanted to get her home, but fuck, this would do just as well.

"Oh, God," she whispered, before taking all of me in her mouth.

"Holy fuck," I mumbled, moving into the slow lane of traffic.

It was so perfect, all over again: her hands and mouth working in tandem, tiny moans vibrating against me and sounding to all the world as if she'd never wanted anything as much as she'd wanted to feel me like this. She started slow, long pulls and tiny teasing licks, looking up at me through dark lashes until I thought I might lose my mind. But she read me like she always did, knowing when not to stop, when to move faster or rougher, squeezing my base tightly. What sent me reeling was her own excitement; her eyes grew dark,

24

pleading, her breath grew labored, and her sounds around me grew more frantic. Too soon, I was gripping the steering wheel, panting and begging, and, finally, cursing loudly as I came in her mouth.

I have no idea how I managed to steer the car onto my street, or pull it into my driveway, but with shaky hands, somehow I got us there. She kissed my navel, and then rested her forehead against my thigh and the car grew completely silent. It wasn't exactly how I imagined being with her again for the first time, but the way it was so hurried and spontaneous . . . that felt like us, too.

When she pushed against my arm so she could sit up, I shifted in my seat, reaching to zip my pants and fasten my belt.

"What the hell?" she asked, looking out the window. Her surprised tone burst through my sex haze. "Is this your house? Why are we here?"

"You wanted to go to your place?"

Shrugging, she said, "I just assumed we would. I don't have any of my things here."

"I don't have anything at your place, either."

"But I have spare toothbrushes. Do you have spare toothbrushes?"

What the fuck is she talking about?

"You can use mine. What the fuck?"

Sighing, she opened her door and mumbled, "Such a man."

"To be clear," I said, getting out of the car and following her up the walkway, *"I brought you here because this is where I was going to bring you after San Diego. I was going to tie you to my headboard and spank the fuck out of you. And I intend that again, after everything you put me through."*

Chloe stopped where she stood on my porch, her back to me for several long, confusing seconds before she turned to stare at me. *"What did you just say?"*

"Did I stutter?" I asked, and when she just continued to stare, I explained, *"Yes, we were apart because I was a jerk. But so were you."*

Her eyes narrowed and grew dark. I was half scared, and half thrilled as fuck that she was about to blow up at me. She backed me to my front door, her fist curling tight around my tie before she yanked down, pulling me so our faces were nearly even. Her dark eyes were wild and wide. *"Give me your keys."*

Reaching into my pocket, I pulled them out, depositing them in her waiting palm without question.

I watched as she flipped through them and actually found the right key on the first guess. *"It's the top lock and the—"*

She cut me off with a fingertip to my lips. *"Shh. No talking."*

I tried to puzzle out what was happening. Obviously she hadn't expected me to tease her about leaving me the way she did. Maybe she suspected we'd left all of that discussion in the conference room where we reunited. And I suppose in many ways we had. I didn't need her to apologize, and I didn't feel like I needed to apologize anymore. But our separation had been a shitty few months, so it didn't feel like the conversation about it was entirely over. Besides, spanking her seemed like the most appropriate way to work it all out of our systems.

Her hand didn't fumble behind me as she slipped the key into the lock. I heard the familiar squeak and click, then she pushed the door open and backed me over the threshold.

"Straight back to my living room," I offered. "Or down the hall to my bed."

I could sense her steering me to the living room, her eyes moving between my face, her hand on my tie, and the house behind her. It was, after all, the first time she was seeing my home.

"It's nice," she whispered, seeming to decide what she was doing with me as she pulled me up short. "It's so clean. It's so . . . you."

"Thank you," I said, laughing. "I think."

As if remembering that she was punishing me for something, she threw me a stern look. "Stay here."

She left and although I was tempted to see what she was up to, I followed her instruction. After only a few seconds she returned with one of my high-backed dining room chairs. Once she had it situated behind me, she pressed on my shoulders to urge me to sit down.

Turning, she walked over to my sound system, picked up the remote, and scanned the buttons.

"First turn on the—"

"Shh." Without turning, Chloe held up a single hand to quiet me.

I closed my mouth, jaw tense. She was stretching my patience a little. If she hadn't indicated that I was supposed to stay seated, and I didn't suspect she wanted to play, I would have had her flat on her stomach by then and already yanked her ass in the air for a spanking.

After only a few moments, a smooth, pulsing rhythm slid into the room with a woman's husky voice layered on top. Chloe hesitated at the stereo, shoulders moving with her deep, nervous breaths.

"Baby, come here," I whispered, hoping she heard me over the music.

She turned, returning to me and standing so close that her thighs pressed against my knees. My face was at her chest level, and I couldn't help but lean forward, kiss her breast through her shirt. But her hands came up and pushed my shoulders back so that I was again sitting up straight.

She followed my body, moving to straddle my lap. With both hands, she reached forward and toyed with my tie.

"What you said outside . . . ," she whispered. *"Maybe we do need to talk some more."*

"Okay."

"But if you don't want to do it now, we can go to your room and you can do everything you want to me." She lifted her gaze to my face, dark eyes searching. *"We can talk later."*

"I'll talk about anything you want." I swallowed, and smiled up at her. "Then I'll take you to my bed and do everything I want."

I could hardly catch my breath. I reached up to undo the top button of my shirt, but she caught my hand and pulled it down, her eyebrow raised in silent question.

Slowly, she undid my tie until it was wrapped around her fist like a boxer's tape. I was so turned on by this power in her that when she moved my hands to the side of the chair, I didn't really notice. My cock grew uncomfortably hard, and I shifted my hips to adjust the angle in my pants, my heart pounding beneath my ribs. What the fuck was she going to do?

"Tell me you love me," she whispered.

My heart was racing and my blood seemed to pound through my veins. "I love you. Wildly. I'm . . ." I'd imagined this a thousand different times, but this moment felt way too loaded and my words came out in a breathless rush. Taking a deep breath and closing my eyes, I murmured, "I'm wildly in love with you."

"But you were mad at me when I left."

My stomach tightened. Was this going to turn into a fight? And would that be a good or a bad thing?

Chloe leaned forward, kissed my chin, my lips, my cheek. She slid her mouth to my ear.

And then I felt a tug around my wrists; she had bound my hands behind the chair with my tie. "It's okay," she said. "Don't worry. I just want to talk about it."

She wanted to talk about it, wanted to feel comfortable hearing how it had affected me, how I'd been angry. But she needed me tied up first? I smiled, turning to catch her lips in a kiss.

"Yes, I was mad at you. I was mostly heartbroken, but I was angry, too."

"Tell me why you were mad." Her mouth moved farther away from mine, to my neck, and she sucked along my skin while I considered how to answer.

It felt like our breakup had happened a million years ago, but also like it happened only earlier today. The fact that she was here, straddling my lap and kissing me, reminded me that this was in many ways ancient history. But the way my chest twisted at the memory of her leaving me . . . it felt too close.

"You never let me explain, or apologize. I called. I went over to your place. I would have done anything to work it out."

She didn't say anything, didn't try to defend herself. Instead, she stood and stepped away, bending to unfasten the strap of her heels. She stepped out of them, returning to me, running her fingers into my hair and pulling my face against her chest.

"We knew it wasn't going to be easy to transition from hate-fucking to being in love," I said into the soft fabric of her top. "And the first time I messed up you left me."

She slipped the top button free on her jeans, slowly pulled the zipper down, and then peeled them off her legs. In a few more seconds, her shirt joined her jeans on the floor. She stood before me, completely naked but for her bra and tiny red lace panties. In the shadowed room, her skin looked like silk.

Fuck, fuck, fuck, fuck.

"I'd only realized that I loved you, that maybe I had been in love with you for a while, and then suddenly you were gone." I looked up at her, hoping I hadn't gone too far.

She slid over my lap, and I wanted more than anything to have my hands free to run up her strong thighs. Instead, I stared at where her legs parted over me, just a few inches away from my cock.

"I'm sorry," she whispered. I blinked up in surprise. "I wouldn't change it, because I did what I needed to do at the time. But I know it hurt you, and I know it wasn't fair to just shut you out."

I nodded, tilting my chin so she would come closer and kiss me. Her mouth pressed to mine, soft and wet, and a tiny moan escaped her lips.

"Thank you for coming this morning," she said against me.

"Would you have come to me?" I asked.

"Yes."

"When?"

"Tomorrow morning. After I'd finished my presentation. I'd decided that about a week ago."

I groaned, leaning forward to kiss her. She arched away so instead I kissed her chin, and down her throat.

"Did you see anyone else while we were apart?"

I stopped and gaped up at her. "What—is that a serious question? No."

A smile spread across her face. "I just needed to hear it."

"If you let another man touch you, Chloe, I swear to God, I—"

"Settle down, Trigger." She pressed two fingertips to my mouth. "I didn't."

I closed my eyes, kissing her fingers and nodding. The offending image evaporated slowly from my mind, but my heart didn't seem to slow even a touch.

I felt her breath on my neck just a beat before she asked, "Did you think about me?"

"Several times every minute."

"Did you ever think about fucking me?"

All words slipped from my head. Every word in the English language disappeared and I shifted under her, wanting her so intensely in this vulnerable and open and quiet moment that I feared I would lose it the second she freed me from my pants.

"Not at first," I managed, finally. "But after a few weeks, I tried."

"Tried to touch yourself and think of me? Like your hand could stand in for me?"

I watched her expression grow from curious to predatory before answering, "Yeah."

"Did you come?"

"Jesus, Chloe." How was it so hot to be grilled by her like this?

She didn't blink or fidget at all while waiting for me to answer. She simply stared me down. "Tell me."

I couldn't fight my smile. Always such a ballbuster. "A couple of times. It wasn't very pleasurable because you would come into my head and it was just as frustrating as it was relieving."

"For me, too," she said. "I missed you so much it hurt. At work I missed you. At home, in my bed, I could barely stand it. The only time I could clear you from my head was when I was—"

"Running," I whispered. "I can tell. You lost too much weight."

Her eyebrow lifted. "So did you."

"I also drank too much," I admitted, reminding her that this wasn't a contest. She didn't need to prove she'd fared better. I was actually pretty sure she had. "The first month we were apart is still kind of a blur."

"Sara told me how you looked. She told me I wasn't being fair by staying away from you."

My eyebrows inched up in surprise. Really? Sara had said that? "You did what you needed to do."

Leaning back, she looked down the length of my torso, and then up to my eyes. I was curious to see that she looked a little surprised. Maybe even giddy. "You let me tie you up."

I stared up at her. "Of course I did."

"I just wasn't sure you'd let me. I thought I'd tricked you—I thought you might say no."

"Chloe, you've owned me since the first second I saw you. I'd have let you tie me up back in the conference room if you'd asked."

A tiny smile pulled at one side of her mouth. "I wouldn't have let you if you'd asked."

"Good." I leaned in for a kiss. "You're smarter than I am."

She stood, reaching behind her to unfasten her bra. It slid down her arms and fluttered to the floor. "I think we've both always known that's true."

The way I wanted her was a kind of steady, heavy ache. I was so hard I could feel my every heartbeat through my cock, but I also felt like my vision was oversaturated with color: the red of her panties and lips, the brown of her eyes, the creamy ivory of her skin. My body was screaming for hers to take me inside, but my brain couldn't stop drinking in each detail. "Let me feel you."

She returned to me, lifting her chest to my mouth. I leaned forward, taking a nipple between my lips, flicking it with my tongue. Without warning, she stood and stepped away, turning her back to me and looking over her shoulder with a mischievous smile on her face.

"What are you doing, little devil?" I panted.

Her thumbs hooked into the waist of her lacy panties and she wiggled her hips as she began to lower them.

No. No way in hell.

"Don't you fucking dare," I said, yanking my hands free from her flimsy knot and standing to tower over her like a storm cloud forming in my own living room. "Go down the hall and get on my bed. If you even think of taking off your panties, I will take care of myself and you'll lie there and watch me come."

Her eyes widened into enormous pools of black in the dark room, and without another word she turned and sprinted down the hall to my bedroom.

———

And with that memory in mind, my day was officially shot. That night had been the single most intimate night of my life, and had launched our relationship from *Giving It a Try* into *Fully Committed*. I would never get over the way she turned her vulnerability into quiet command, or the way she let me turn the tables in my bedroom, tie her to my bed and nibble at every inch of her body.

I groaned as I realized I had no idea when we would ever have such a lazy night together again, and picked up my phone.

Lunch? I texted.

Can't, Chloe replied. Meeting with Douglas from noon to three. Shoot me.

I looked at the clock. It was 11:36. I slid my phone back on my desk and returned to the article I was working on for the *Journal*. I was useless and I knew it.

After about two minutes, I picked up my phone, texting her again, this time using our secret code. Bat signal.

She replied immediately: On my way.

———

The outer door opened and closed, bringing the sound of Chloe's heels tapping across the floor of the office just outside mine. It had once been Chloe's, but when she'd returned to Ryan Media Group after finishing her MBA, she moved to an office of her own in the east wing. End result: the outer office now remained empty. I'd attempted working with a few different assistants, but they never really worked out. Andrea cried all the time. Jesse tapped her pen on her desk and the effect was much like a woodpecker going at a tree. Bruce couldn't type.

Apparently Chloe was more of a saint for "putting up with me" than I'd given her credit for.

My door opened and she stepped through, brows drawn together. We used the bat signal primarily to notify each other of work crises, and for a moment I wondered whether I was overreacting.

"What happened?" she asked, stopping about a foot away from me, her arms crossed over her chest. I could see she was preparing for a professional battle on my behalf, but I wanted her to fight a far more personal one.

"Nothing work related," I said, rubbing my jaw. "I . . ."

I drifted off, staring at each part of her face in turn: her eyes as they narrowed in concentration, the full lips she'd pulled together in concern, her smooth skin. And, of course, I let my eyes drop to her breasts because she'd pushed them together and . . . well, *fuck*.

"Are you looking at my chest?"

"Yes."

"You sent me the bat signal so you could look at my tits?"

"Settle down, firecracker. I sent you the bat signal because I miss you."

Her arms fell to her sides and seemed to stutter, fingers fumbling to straighten the hem of her sweater. "How can you miss me? I stayed over last night."

"I know." I knew this side of her. Forever knee-jerking back to self-preservation.

"And we had all weekend together."

"Yeah, you and me—and Julia and Scott," I reminded her. "And Henry and Mina. Not alone. Not nearly as much as we'd anticipated."

Chloe turned her head and looked out the window. For the first time in weeks we had a perfect, sunny day, and I wanted to take her outside and just . . . sit.

"I feel like I miss you all the time lately," she whispered.

The knot in my chest unwound a bit. "Do you?"

Nodding, she turned back to me. "Your travel schedule sucks right now." She leaned forward, cocked an eyebrow. "And you didn't kiss me goodbye this morning."

"I did, in fact," I said, smiling. "You were still sleeping."

"Doesn't count."

"Are you looking for a fight, Miss Mills?"

She shrugged, struggling to repress a smile as she studied me carefully.

"We could skip the fight and you could just suck on my dick for ten minutes or so."

Without another beat passing, she stepped close and slid her arms around me, stretching to press her face into my neck. "I love you," she whispered. "And I love that you sent the bat signal just because you missed me."

I was struck silent, for probably too long, and I finally managed to croak out an "I love you, too."

It wasn't that Chloe wasn't expressive; she *was*. When we were alone, she was—physically—the most expressive woman I'd ever known. But whereas I told her often how I felt, I could count on two hands the number of times she'd actually said the words "I love you." I didn't need her to say it more, but each time she had, it affected me more profoundly than I'd anticipated.

"Seriously, though," I whispered, struggling to regain my composure. "Maybe I just need a quickie over the desk."

She laughed, shaking her head against my neck and reaching between us to palm my cock. I knew this game, and it was entirely possible she was going to do something mildly threatening that would thrill me as much as it terrified me. But instead of looking at me with danger in her eyes, she turned her head to suck on my neck, whispering, "I can't smell like sex in this meeting with Douglas."

"You think you don't always smell like sex?"

"I don't always smell like *you*," she clarified, before licking my neck.

"The hell you don't."

It had been so long since we'd fooled around in the office, and I was so keen to feel her; I wanted to tear my pants down my legs and shove her skirt over her hips, then ruin the neat stacks of paper on my desk by throwing her down on it.

Mercifully, she kissed from my jaw down my neck and slid along my body to the floor, pulling her skirt up slightly, demurely, so she could kneel in front of me.

But no . . . once on the floor, she kept pulling her skirt up until it bunched at her hips. With one hand, she reached between her legs; with the other, she made quick work of my belt and zipper. I closed my eyes, needing to calm my mind for a beat as she freed me quickly, and without hesitation pulled my cock into her mouth. I'd been nearly hard, and with her touch I lengthened. Warm, wet suction slid down my length and back up again, harder with the second pass as she adjusted to the feel of me in her mouth.

I felt her breath come out in little bursts against my navel, could hear the sound of her fingers moving over herself as she kneeled on the floor.

"Are you touching yourself?"

Her head shifted slightly as she nodded.

"Were you already wet for me?"

She stilled for a beat, and then reached her hand up over her head. Bending down, I sucked two of her fingers into my mouth.

Fuck.

It obliterated me to see so clearly how much she wanted this. I knew from experience how she tasted before she was truly ready for me—for example, when I came over late and surprised her in her sleep with my mouth on her—and I knew how differently she tasted after we'd teased each other for what felt like an eternity. This, on her fingers, was full arousal, and it sent my head spinning. How long had she been thinking of this? All day? Since I left this morning? But she didn't let me linger over it too long, returning her hand quickly to the unseen space between her legs.

I watched her head move, her lips slide over my length, and tried to let it calm me. But even when her mouth was on me like this or I was buried inside her, I'd always want *more*. It was impossible to have her every way at once, but it never stopped me from imagining it: a whirlwind of positions and sounds and my hands in her hair and on her hips, my fingers in her mouth and yet also between her legs and pulling on the back of her thighs.

When I ran my hands into her hair she knew I wanted faster, and when my hips started to jerk she knew not to tease, not even a little. At least, not since she had a meeting any minute.

In a sudden flash I remembered that my office was unlocked; Chloe had come in here thinking we'd discuss work. The outer office was closed but not locked, either.

"Oh, shit," I groaned, because somehow the idea that we could be caught made it so much hotter. "*Chloe—*" Without more warning, my orgasm barreled down my spine, sharp and warm, and so intense it made my legs shake and my fists curl tightly in her hair. She arched against the pull, her arm jerking as she touched herself, causing the sounds of her own pleasure to come out muffled around me.

Looking down, I realized she was watching my reaction . . . of course she was. Her eyes were wide, but somehow soft, and she looked *fascinated*. I'm sure her expression was exactly how mine was every time I'd seen her come apart under my touch. After a pause to catch my breath, I pulled out from her mouth and kneeled on the floor facing her, reaching to cup one of my hands over the one she had between her legs. She shifted a little, letting my fingers take over. I slid two of them inside, pushing and deep, and she almost toppled backward, her body clamping down around me. Steadying her with my other hand on her hip, I pressed a kiss to her lips, humming at the way they were a little red, a little swollen.

"I'm really close," she said, slipping her free hand around my neck for support.

"I like how you think you need to tell me that."

I kept waiting for my touch to seem overly familiar, or my technique to grow tired, but each time she felt the sweep and press of my thumb against her clit it seemed more intense than the time before.

"Another," she managed in a tight voice. "Please, I want . . ."

She never finished her thought. She didn't need to. I pumped three fingers into her and watched as her head fell back, her lips parted, and the quiet, husky sound of her trying-to-be-quiet orgasm raced through her.

For a few seconds, she let me hold her up, breathe in the scent of her hair, and pretend that we were somewhere else, maybe my living room or her bedroom, certainly not on the floor of my unlocked office.

Seeming to remember this at the same time I did, Chloe pulled up her panties and slid her skirt back down her thighs before letting me take her hand to help her stand. As usual, I was struck by the quiet all around us, and wondered if we were ever as controlled and sneaky as we thought we were.

She looked around, a little dazed, and then tossed me a lazy grin. "This will make it even harder to stay awake in my meeting."

"Not sorry," I murmured, bending down to kiss her neck.

When I straightened, she turned and walked into my washroom, pushing the sleeves of her sweater up her forearms so she could clean her hands. I stepped close, pressing my front to her back, and moved my hands under the water with hers. Soap slid between our fingers and she leaned her head back against my chest. I wanted to spend an hour washing her scent from our fingers just so I could stand this close.

"Are we staying at your place tonight?" I asked. It was always a hard choice. My bed was better for play, but her kitchen was better stocked.

She turned off the water and reached to dry her hands on my towel. "Your place. I have to do laundry."

"Don't ever let me hear you say romance is dead." I took my turn with the towel and then bent to kiss her. She kept her mouth closed, eyes open, and I pulled back a little.

"Bennett?"

"Mmm?"

"I do, you know."

"You do what?"

"Love you. Maybe I don't tell you enough. Maybe that's why you used the bat signal."

I smiled, my heart squeezing tightly beneath my ribs. "I know you do. And that isn't why I texted. I texted because I don't get enough of your exclusive attention lately and I'm a greedy bastard. Hasn't my mother warned you that I've never been good at sharing?"

"After we move to New York, things will quiet down and we'll have more time."

"In *New York*? Doubtful," I said. "And even if things do

settle down, wouldn't it be nice to get away for a little bit before all that anyway?"

"When?" she asked, and looked around as if her packed calendar permeated every surface.

"There won't ever be a perfect time. And when we move offices, it will be even crazier for a while."

Laughing, she shook her head. "Well, I can't think of a worse time. Maybe late summer?" With a quick kiss, she turned and grabbed her phone from my desk, eyes widening when she saw the time. "I have to go," she said, kissing me once more before leaving my office.

And the topic was dismissed.

But the word *vacation* stayed in my mind.

Three

I'd had big plans for tonight: make dinner, eat dinner *together*, finally decide which apartment we were going to rent in New York, discuss what to keep from both his place and mine, figure out when in the hell we'd find time to pack it all in the first place.

Oh, and spend the remaining eight hours relearning every inch of my Beautiful Bastard's body. Twice.

But that itinerary was before he'd walked through the door of his house to find me cooking dinner in his kitchen. Before he'd tossed his jacket and keys to the couch and practically sprinted across the room. Before he pulled me back against him and sucked at the skin below my ear as if he hadn't tasted me in weeks.

Needless to say, the plan had been downsized dramatically.

One: dinner. Two: naked.

Even so, Bennett seemed inclined to skip steps.

"We're never going to eat at this rate," I said, tilting my head back as he kissed along my neck. His warm breath curled over my skin and the knife I'd been hold-ing clattered to the cutting board.

"And?" he whispered, pressing his hips to my ass be-fore turning me to face him.

The cabinets were hard against my back. Bennett was harder against my front. He bent down, towering over me without the benefit of my shoes, and brushed his lips over my throat.

"And . . ." I mumbled. "Food is overrated."

He laughed softly, hands skimming my sides to rest at my hips. "Exactly. And God, it feels like I haven't touched you in weeks."

"This afternoon," I corrected, pulling back just enough to meet his eyes. "It was this afternoon, you know—when I sucked you off at your desk?"

"Oh, yes. I seem to remember something like that. It's a little hazy, though. Perhaps you could refresh my memory . . . tongue, cock . . ."

"Nice mouth, Ryan. Does your mother know you're such a pig?"

He barked out a laugh. "If the way she looked at us after we fucked in the coatroom at my cousin's wed-ding in February is any indication, then yes."

"I hadn't seen you in two weeks!" I said, feeling my cheeks warm. "Don't look so smug, you ass."

"But I'm *your* ass," he said, and pressed a lingering kiss to my lips. "Don't pretend like you don't love it."

I couldn't argue. Bennett might have spent more time out of Chicago than in it lately, but he was all mine. He never left any doubt about that. "And speaking of asses"—he reached down and squeezed mine, hard— "the things I'm going to do to yours tonight . . ."

I started to reply—to argue or say something smart in return that would put me back in the verbal driver's seat—but I couldn't think of anything.

"Jesus. You've been stunned silent," he said, eyes wide in surprise. "If I'd known that's all it'd take to get a little peace and quiet, I'd have brought it up ages ago."

"I . . . um." I opened and closed my mouth a few times but nothing came out. This was new. When the oven timer cut through the air, I forced myself to pull away, still a little off balance.

I pulled the bread from the oven and drained the pasta, feeling Bennett move up behind me again. He hooked his chin over my shoulder, wrapped his arms around my waist.

"You smell so good," he said. His mouth went back to work on my neck, as his hands began a slow descent down to the hem of my skirt. I was more than a little tempted to let him finish.

Instead, I nodded to the cutting board. "Can you finish the salad for me, please?"

He groaned and loosened his tie, grunting something unintelligible as he began working at the opposite counter.

Ribbons of garlic-scented steam curled up from the bowl as I tossed the pasta and sauce together, trying to clear my head. As usual, it was impossible when he was nearby. There was just something about Bennett Ryan that seemed to suck all the air out of a room.

I'd been blindsided by how hard I'd fallen for him, and lately I missed him so much when he was gone. Sometimes I'd talk to my empty bedroom. "How was your day?" I'd ask. "My new assistant is hilarious," I'd say. Or: "Has my apartment always been this quiet?"

Other days, when I'd worn his shirt to sleep so many times it had lost his smell, I'd go over to his place. I'd sit in the huge chair that looked out over the lake, and wonder what he was doing. Wonder if it was possible for him to miss me even a fraction as much as I missed him. Jesus. I never used to understand women who acted like this when their boyfriends traveled. I used to just assume it was a good opportunity for a full night's sleep and some downtime.

Somehow, Bennett had managed to work his way into every part of my life. He was still the same stubborn, driven man he'd always been, and I loved that he hadn't changed who he was just because we were together. He treated me as an equal, and even though

I knew he loved me more than anything, he never cut me any slack. For that I loved him even more.

I carried our plates to the table and glanced back over my shoulder. Bennett was still grumbling to himself as he sliced a tomato.

"Are you still complaining?" I asked.

"Of course." He brought the salad over, smacking my ass before pulling out my chair.

He poured us each a glass of wine before dropping into the seat across from me. Bennett watched me take a sip, his eyes moving from mine, to my lips, and back up again. A sweet smile pulled at the corner of his mouth, but then he seemed to blink back into focus, remembering something. "I've been meaning to ask you, how's Sara?"

Sara Dillon had graduated from the same MBA program that I had, but had since left RMG to work for another firm. She was one of my best friends, and Bennett had offered her the Director of Finance position in the new branch but she'd turned him down, not wanting to leave her family and the life she had in Chicago. He didn't blame her, of course, but as the big day drew closer and we still hadn't found anyone, I knew he was beginning to worry.

I shrugged, remembering the conversation I'd had with her earlier that day. Sara's douchebag of a fiancé had been photographed kissing another woman, and it seemed Sara might really be seeing what the rest of us had suspected for years: Andy was a cheating dick.

"She's okay, I guess. Andy still claims he was set up. The other woman's name still pops up in the paper every week. You know Sara. She's not going to show the world how she feels, but I can tell she's completely shattered over this."

He hummed, considering. "Think she's finally done? No more taking him back?"

"Who knows? They've been together since she was twenty-one. If she hasn't left him by now then maybe she'll stay with him forever."

"Wish I'd gone with my gut and knocked him on his ass at the Smith House event last month. What a miserable sleaze."

"I've tried to talk her into coming to New York but . . . she's so stubborn."

"Stubborn? I can't possibly see why the two of you are friends," he deadpanned.

I threw a cherry tomato at him.

The rest of the meal was all talk about work, about getting the new office off the ground and all the pieces that still needed to be put into place before that could happen. We'd begun discussing whether his family would be going back to New York again before the new offices opened when I asked, "When did your dad get back in town?"

I waited a moment, but when Bennett didn't answer, I looked up, surprised to see him pushing his food around his plate.

"Everything okay over there, Ryan?"

A few seconds of silence passed before he said, "I miss you working for me."

I felt my eyes widen. "What?"

"I know. It doesn't make any sense to me, either. We were awful to each other, and it was an impossible situation." Holy crap, what an understatement. The fact that we managed to survive working in the same office together for ten months without bloodshed or some sort of manslaughter stapler incident *still* surprised me. "But . . . ," he continued, looking up at me from across the table, "I saw you every day. It was predictable. Consistent. I pushed and you pushed back. It was the most fun I've ever had at a job. And I took it for granted."

I set my glass down and met his eyes, feeling an overwhelming surge of affection for this man. "That . . . makes sense," I said, searching for the right words. "I don't think I appreciated what it meant to see you every day, either. Even if I did want to poison you on no less than twenty-seven separate occasions."

"Ditto," he replied with a smirk. "And sometimes I

feel guilty for how many times I threw you out the window in my fantasies. But I most certainly plan on making it up to you." He picked up his glass, took a long drink.

"Do you now?"

"Yep. I have a list."

I raised an eyebrow in silent question.

"Well, first I'm going to peel off that skirt." He bent to glance under the table. "I'd hassle you for wearing that lacy stuff underneath just to torture me, but we both know I'm into that kind of thing."

I watched as he straightened and leaned back in his chair, hands clasped behind his head. The weight of his attention brought goose bumps to my skin. Anyone else would have been intimidated—I could still remember a time when I was—but right now all I felt was adrenaline, a thrill that shot through my chest and settled warm and heavy in my stomach.

"And that sweater," he began, eyes on my chest now. "I'd like to rip it open, hear the sound of those little buttons as they pop off and scatter across the floor."

I crossed my legs, swallowed. He followed the movement, a smile slowly lifting at the corners of his mouth.

"Then maybe I'd spread you out on this table." He leaned over, made a show of testing its sturdiness. "Put your legs over my shoulders, suck on you until you're just *begging* for my cock."

I tried to seem unaffected, tried to break from his

stare. I couldn't. I cleared my throat, my mouth suddenly dry. "You could have done that last night," I said, teasing him.

"No. Last night we were tired and I just wanted to feel you come. Tonight, I want to take my time, undress you, kiss every inch of that body—fuck you. Watch you fuck me."

Was it suddenly getting warm in here?

"Pretty sure of yourself, aren't you?" I asked.

"Most definitely."

"And what makes you think I don't have a list of my own?" I stood, dessert forgotten as I rounded the table to stop in front of him. His cock was already stiff, straining against the fly of his pants. He followed my gaze and smirked up at me, pupils dark and so wide they drowned the hazel surrounding them.

I wanted to rip off my clothes and feel the heat of that stare on my skin, wake up in the morning exhausted and sore and with the memory of his fingertips still pressing into my body. How did he make me feel this way with just a look and a few dirty words?

Bennett shifted in his chair and I stepped between his legs, reaching out to push the hair—that eternally freshly fucked hair—from his forehead. The soft strands slipped between my fingers and I tilted his head back, bringing his eyes to mine. *I've missed you so much*, I wanted to say. *Stay. Don't go so far away. I love you.*

The words stuck in my throat and nothing more than a "Hi" slipped out instead.

Bennett tilted his head, smile widening as he looked up at me. "Hi." Warm hands gripped my hips, pulled me closer. Laughter curled around the single word and I knew he could read me like a book, saw every thought as clearly as if it were written across my forehead in ink. It's not that I wasn't comfortable saying I loved him, it's just that it was so new. I'd never said it to anyone before him, and sometimes it felt scary, like opening up my chest and handing him my heart.

His hand moved up to rest on my breast, thumb brushing along the underside. "I can't help but wonder what's under this pretty little sweater," he said.

I sucked in a breath, felt my nipples harden beneath the thin cashmere. He slipped one button through the hole, and then another, until the cardigan fell open and his eyes moved over my barely-there bra. He hummed in appreciation. "This is new."

"And expensive. *Don't* ruin it," I warned.

He couldn't contain his smug smile. "I would never."

"You bought me a four-hundred-dollar slip and then used it to tie me to your bed, Bennett."

He laughed, pushing the sweater from my shoulders, taking his time to unwrap me like a gift. Long fingers moved to the waist of my skirt and the soft sound of the zipper filled the room. He did as he'd promised, purposefully peeling the wool from my hips and down my legs to pool at my feet, leaving me in only my lace bra and rather skimpy panties.

The air conditioner switched on and a low whir carried through the apartment, a burst of cool air rushing along my exposed skin. Bennett pulled me down onto his lap, my legs on either side of his hips. The rough fabric of his pants brushed against the backs of my bare thighs, my practically naked ass. I should have felt vulnerable like this—with me in so little and him fully dressed—but I relished it. It was so much like our first night together at his home, after my presentation, after we'd both admitted we didn't want to be without the other and he let me tie him up so I could have the nerve to hear how much I'd hurt him.

And then I realized this position was intentional. I suspected he was thinking about that exact night, too. His eyes shone with such hunger, such adoration, that I couldn't help but feel a sense of power, like there wasn't anything this man wouldn't do if I just asked.

I reached for the buttons of his shirt, wanting him naked and over me, behind me—everywhere. I wanted to taste him, scratch marks into his skin, and connect them with my fingers, my lips and my teeth. I wanted to stretch him out on the table and fuck him until any thought of either of us ever leaving this room was a distant memory.

Somewhere in the apartment, a phone rang. We froze,

neither of us saying anything, both waiting, hoping it had been a fluke and that nothing but silence would follow. But the shrill ringtone—one I'd become all too familiar with—filled the air again. Work. The emergency ringtone. And not the regular emergency one—the *emergency*-emergency one. Bennett swore, resting his forehead against my chest. My heart pounded beneath my ribs and my breaths felt too quick, too loud.

"Fuck, I'm sorry," he said when it continued to ring. "I have to—"

"I know." I stood, using the back of the chair to support my shaky legs.

Bennett scrubbed his hands over his face before he stood and crossed the room, finding his phone where he'd slung his jacket over the back of the couch. "Yeah," he said, and then listened.

I bent for my sweater and slipped it over my shoulders, found my skirt and pulled it up my hips. I carried the dishes into the kitchen while he talked. I was trying to give him some sense of privacy but grew concerned as his voice continued to rise.

"What do you mean *they can't find it*?" he shouted. I leaned against the doorway and watched as he paced back and forth in front of the wide wall of windows. "This is happening tomorrow and someone's *misplaced* the fucking *master file*? Can't someone else handle this?" A pause ensued in which I swear I actually watched Bennett's blood pressure rise. *"Are you kidding?"* Another pause. Bennett closed his eyes tight and took a deep breath. "Fine. I'll be there in twenty."

When he ended the call, it took a moment for him to look at me.

"It's okay," I said.

"It's not."

He was right. It wasn't okay. It sucked. "Can't someone else handle it?"

"Who? I can't trust something this important to those incompetent assholes. The Timbk2 account launches tomorrow and the marketing team can't find the file with the financial specs—" He stopped and shook his head, reached for his jacket. "God, we need someone in New York who knows what the fuck they're doing. I'm so sorry, Chlo."

Bennett knew how much we needed tonight, but he also had a job to do. I knew this better than anyone.

"Go," I said, closing the distance between us. "I'll be right here when you're done." I handed him his keys and stood up on my toes to kiss him.

"In my bed?"

I nodded.

"Wear my shirt."

"Only your shirt."

"I love you."

I grinned. "I know. Now go save the world."

Four

You have got to be fucking kidding me.

I turned the key in the ignition and revved the engine hard enough for the RPMs to hit red. I wanted to peel out and tear down the street, leaving the sign of my frustration as black tire marks on the road.

I was tired. *Fuck* was I tired, and I hated to have to clean up other people's messes at work. I'd been working twelve-, fifteen-, hell, even eighteen-hour days for months, and the one night I was able to put aside time with Chloe at home, I was called in.

I paused as the word seemed to bounce around inside of my skull: *home.*

Whether we were at my place or hers, out with friends, or in that tiny little shithole Chinese restaurant she liked so much, it felt like home to me. The strangest part was that the house that had cost me a fortune had *never* felt like home until she spent time there. Was her home also with *me*?

We hadn't even had time to pick where we would *live* in New York. We had identified the new location for RMG, made a map of where each of our offices would be, drawn up blue-prints of the renovations and hired a designer . . . but Chloe and I didn't have an apartment to go to.

Which was the greatest sign that old habits die hard, because in reality my relationship with her had completely altered my relationship to my job. Only a year ago I'd been committed to one thing: my career. Now, the thing that mattered most to me was Chloe, and every time my career got in the way of being with her it burned me up inside. I don't even know specifically when that had happened, but I suspect the change had been effected long before I would have ever admitted it. Maybe it was the night Joel came to my parents' house for dinner. Or maybe it was the next day, when I fell on my knees in front of her and apologized the only way I knew how. Most likely it was even earlier than all of that, on the first night I kissed her roughly in the conference room, in my darkest, weakest moment. Thank God I'd been such an idiot.

I glanced down at the clock on my dashboard and the date, backlit in red, hit me like a fist to the chest: May 5. Exactly one year ago, I'd watched Chloe walk off the plane from San Diego, her shoulders set in hurt and anger at how I'd essentially thrown her under the bus after she'd covered for me with a client. The next day she'd resigned; she'd left me. I blinked, trying to clear the memory from my mind. She came back, I reminded myself. We'd worked it out in the past eleven months, and despite all of my frustration with my work schedule, I'd *never* been happier. She was the only woman I'd ever want.

I thought back to my previous breakup, with Sylvie almost two years ago now. Our relationship started the way one climbs on an escalator: with a single step and then moving without effort along a single path. We started out friendly and easily slipped into physical intimacy. The situation worked perfectly for me because she provided companion-ship and sex, and she'd never asked for more than I offered. When we broke up, she admitted she knew I wouldn't give her more, and for a while the sex and quasi-intimacy had been enough. Until, for her, they weren't anymore.

After a long embrace and one final kiss, I'd let her go. I'd gone straight to my favorite restaurant for a quiet din-ner alone, and then headed to bed early, where I slept the entire night without waking once. No drama. No heartbreak. It ended and I closed the door on that part of my life, com-pletely ready to move on. Three months later, I was back in Chicago.

It was comical to compare that to the reaction I'd had to losing Chloe. I'd essentially turned into a filthy hobo, not eat-ing, not showering, and surviving entirely on scotch and self-pity. I remembered clutching to the tiny details Sara would share with me about Chloe—how she was doing, how she looked—and trying to determine from these tidbits whether she missed me and could possibly be as miserable as I was.

The day Chloe returned to RMG was, coincidentally, Sara's

last day at the firm. Although we had made up, Chloe had insisted that she sleep at her place and I sleep at mine so that we would actually get some rest. After a chaotic morning, I walked into the break room to find Chloe snacking on a small pack of almonds, reading some marketing reports. Sara was heating up leftovers in the tiny microwave, having refused our entreaties to give her a big sendoff lunch. I came in to pour myself a cup of coffee, and the three of us stood together in loaded silence for what felt like fifteen minutes.

I'd finally broken it.

"Sara," I said, and my voice felt too loud in the silent room. Her eyes turned to me, wide and clear. "Thank you for coming to me that first day Chloe was gone. Thank you for giving me whatever updates you could. For that, and other reasons, I'm sorry to see you go."

She shrugged, smoothing her bangs to the side and giving me a small smile. "I'm just glad to see you two together again. Things have been way too quiet around here. And by quiet I mean boring. And by boring I mean nobody screaming or calling each other a hateful shrew." She coughed and took an almost comically loud slurp from her drink.

Chloe groaned. "No chance of that anymore, I assure you." She popped an almond into her mouth. "He may not be my boss anymore, but he's still most definitely a screamer."

Laughing, I stole a peek at her ass as she stood and bent down to pull a bottle of water out of the bottom shelf of the fridge.

"Still," I said, turning back to Sara. "I appreciate that you kept me up to date. I would have probably lost my mind otherwise."

Sara's eyes softened and, as she fidgeted, I could tell she was a little uncomfortable in the face of my rare display of emotion. "Like I said, I'm glad it worked out. These things are worth fighting for." She lifted her chin and gave Chloe one last smile before leaving the room.

That giddiness I'd felt after Chloe's return made it easy to ignore the whispers that followed us through the halls of Ryan Media Group. I had my office and she had hers now, and we were each determined to prove to ourselves as much as anyone else that we could do this.

We'd lasted almost an hour apart.

"I missed you," she said, slipping into my office and closing the door behind her. "Do you think they'll give me my old office back?"

"No. Much as I like the idea, at this point it would be blatantly inappropriate."

"I was only half serious." She rolled her eyes and then paused, looking around. I could almost see each memory coming back to her: when she'd spread her legs across the desk from me, when she'd let me make her come with my fingers to distract her from her worries, and, I imagine, each time we'd sat together in this office, not saying everything we could have said so much sooner.

"I love you," I said. "I've loved you for a long time."

She blinked up and then moved close, stretching to kiss me. And then she pulled me into the bathroom and begged me to make love to her against the wall, at noon on a Monday.

As I pulled into the parking deck at the offices and turned into my spot, I remembered Sara's words. Shutting off the car, I stared at the concrete wall in front of me. *These things are worth fighting for.* Sara had taken her own advice home to Chicago's most deplorable womanizer. She'd looked out for me when she knew I was broken and lost without Chloe. In contrast, I'd let Sara continue on with a man I knew was unfaithful, all because I felt it wasn't my place to interfere. Where would I be if Sara had done the same?

Contemplating what that said about me, I climbed from the car and into the main lobby. The night security guard waved, then went back to his newspaper as I headed to the elevators. The building was so empty I could hear every creak and click of the machine around me. Wheels whirred along cables and the car gave a quiet thud as it settled on the eighteenth floor.

I knew no one else was here. The team was scrambling to find the newest version of the file, and in their panic were probably scouring their local document files on their laptops. I doubted anyone had thought to come in and check the work server.

In the end I'd had to leave Chloe for what amounted to twenty-three minutes of work, which effectively guaranteed my mood tomorrow would be thunderous. I hated having to do someone else's job. The contract had been mislabeled and—exactly as I had suspected—put into the wrong folder on the server. In fact, a hard copy was sitting faceup on my desk, where someone actually competent might have noticed it and spared me this trip to the office. I forwarded the file to one of my executives in Marketing and made several copies of the document itself, highlighting the parties on the first page and pointedly placing one on the desk of every person involved in the account, before finally leaving the office. It was, in a way, kind of dickish of me to be so precise. But then, this was what they earned when they pulled me away from Chloe.

I knew these small inconveniences got me too worked up, but it was this type of detail that defined a team. Which was exactly why I needed someone on top of their game for New York. I groaned as I dropped back into my car and started the engine, knowing this was just one more thing I needed to accomplish in the next month.

In my current mood, I was in no state to return to Chloe. I'd only be surly and irritable . . . and not really in the fun way.

God, I just wanted to *be with her*. Why did it have to be so fucking difficult? I had so few hours with Chloe as it was, and I didn't want to waste them because I was stressed about work and apartment hunting and finding someone who could just do their fucking job without being babysat.

We'd complained about not seeing enough of each other, of working too hard, why didn't we just . . . fix it? Go away? I knew Chloe thought the timing was all wrong, but when would it ever be right? Nobody was going to just hand it to us and since when had I ever been the type of person who waited for something to come along anyway?

Fuck that. Fix it.

"Get your shit together, Ben." My voice rang out in the quiet interior of my car, and after a brief glace to the clock to make sure I wasn't calling too late, I reached for my phone, scrolling to the correct number before hitting dial. I pulled out of the parking spot and turned onto Michigan Avenue.

After about six rings, Max's voice boomed from the car speakers. "Oi, Ben!"

I smiled, accelerating away from work and headed toward one of the most familiar places on earth to me. "Max, how are you?"

"Good, mate. Very bloody good. What's this rumor I hear of you lot moving out to the big city?"

I nodded, answering, "We'll be there in a little over a month. Getting set up at Fifth and Fiftieth."

"Close by. Perfect. We'll have to get together when you get to town . . ." He trailed off.

"Definitely, definitely." I hesitated, knowing Max was probably wondering why I was calling him at eleven thirty at night on a Tuesday. "Look, Max, I have a bit of a favor to ask."

"Let's have it."

"I'd like to take my girlfriend away for a bit, and—"

"Girlfriend?" His laughter filled my car.

I laughed, too. I was fairly certain I'd never introduced anyone to Max that way. "Chloe, yes. We both work for RMG and have been slammed lately with the Papadakis campaign. It's rolling quite nicely now, and we maybe have some wiggle room before we move . . ." I hesitated, feeling the words bubble up inside me. "Would I be insane to hire someone to pack up our life here, find us a place in New York, and just . . . *leave* for a few weeks? Just get the hell out of town?"

"That doesn't sound mental, Ben. It sounds like the best way to keep yourself sorted."

"I think so, too. And I know it's impulsive, but I was thinking of taking Chloe to France. I was wondering if you still had the house in Marseille, and if so, whether we could rent it for a few weeks."

Max was laughing quietly. "Fuck yeah, it's still mine. But forget renting it—just have at it. I'll send you the directions straightaway. I'll have Inès go by and clean up for you. The place has been empty since I was there over the winter holidays." He paused. "When were you thinking of heading out?"

The vise that seemed to grip my chest loosened immeasurably as the plan began to solidify in my head. "This weekend?"

"Shit yeah, I'll get on it. Send me your flight details when you have them. I'll call her in the morning and make sure she's there to give you the keys."

"This is fantastic. Thank you, Max. I owe you."

I could practically hear his sly grin when he said, "I'll remember that."

Feeling relaxed for the first time in ages, I turned up the music and let myself imagine getting on a plane with Chloe, nothing ahead of us but sunshine, long mornings spent naked in bed, and some of the best food and wine the world had ever conjured up.

But I had one more stop to make. I knew it was late to go to my parents', but I had no choice. My mind was spinning with plans, and I couldn't head to bed until every last detail had been sorted out.

On the twenty-minute drive to their house, I called and left a message for my travel agent. Then I left a message on my brother Henry's work voice mail that I was leaving for three weeks. I didn't even let myself imagine his reaction. We had a new office, we had everything at work sorted, and we could leave the business of packing up to someone else. I left a message for each of my senior managers letting them know the plan and what I expected each of them to handle in my absence. And then I rolled down all of the windows and let the cool night air whip around me, taking all of my stress with it.

———

Pulling up in front of my parents' house, I laughed thinking back on the first time Chloe and I had come here together as a couple.

It was three days after her presentation to the scholarship board. Two of those days we'd scarcely left my home or my bed. But after the constant calls and texts from my family asking us to come over, for me to let *them* share some time with Chloe, we agreed to a dinner at my parents' house. Everyone had missed her.

We talked on the drive, laughing and teasing, my free hand entwined with one of hers. Absently, she ran the index finger of her other hand in small circles over the top of my wrist, as if reassuring herself that it was real, that I was real, that we were. We hadn't faced the world outside yet, other than that night out with her girlfriends following her presentation. The transition would no doubt be at least a little awkward. But I would never have expected Chloe to be anxious about any of it. She'd always faced every challenge with her own brand of bullheaded fearlessness.

It was only when we stood on the porch and I reached to open their front door that I realized her hand inside mine was shaking.

"What's wrong?" I pulled my hand back, turned her to face me.

She rolled her shoulders. "Nothing. I'm good."

"Unconvincing."

She threw me an annoyed look. "I'm fine. Just open the door."

"Holy shit," I said on an exhale, stunned. "Chloe Mills is actually nervous."

This time she turned to glare up at me fully. "You spotted that? Christ, you're brilliant. Someone should make you a COO and give you a big fancy office." She reached to open the door herself.

I stopped her hand from turning the knob and a grin spread across my face. "Chloe?"

"I just haven't seen them since before . . . you know. And they saw you when you were all . . ." She made a gesture around me, which I gathered was meant to indicate "when Bennett was a complete disaster, after Chloe left him."

"Just . . . let's not make this a thing. I'm fine," she went on.

"I'm just enjoying the rare sighting of a jittery Chloe. Give me a second, let me savor this."

"Fuck off."

"Fuck off?" I stepped in front of her, moved until her body pressed into mine. "Are you trying to seduce me, Miss Mills?"

Finally, she laughed, her shoulders surrendering their tense determination. "I just don't want it to be—"

The front door flew open, and Henry took a step forward, enveloping Chloe in a massive hug. "There she is!"

Chloe peeked up at me over my brother's shoulder and

laughed. "—awkward," she finished, wrapping her arms around him.

Just inside the doorway stood my parents, wearing the biggest shit-eating grins I'd ever seen. My mom's eyes were suspiciously misty.

"It's been way too long," Henry said, releasing my girlfriend and looking right at me.

Groaning inwardly, I registered that this entire night could very easily turn into a giant recap of what a trial this whole thing had been for Chloe, of how impossible I'd been to work with; the details of Miss Mills's challenging attitude would be whitewashed for history.

It was a good thing she looked so damn fit in her little black dress. I'd need the distraction.

I'd called Dad the morning of Chloe's presentation, telling him I'd planned to attend and convince her to present the Papadakis slides. I told him, too, that I was going to ask her to take me back. As usual, Dad had been supportive, but guarded, telling me that no matter what Chloe said, he was proud of me for going after what I wanted.

What I wanted now stepped into the house and hugged my mother, and my father, before looking up at me. "I don't know what I was worried about," she whispered.

"Were you nervous?" Mom asked, eyes wide.

"I just left so abruptly. I've felt bad about that, and about not seeing either of you for months . . ." Chloe trailed off.

"No, no, no, no—you had to put up with Bennett," Henry said, ignoring my irritated sigh. "Trust us, we get it."

"Come on," I groaned, pulling her back. "We don't need to make this a thing."

"I just knew," Mom whispered, putting her hands on Chloe's face. "I knew."

"What the hell, Mom?" I stepped closer, hugging her first and giving her a scowl second. "You 'knew' this even when you set her up with Joel?"

"I think the phrase is 'shit or get off the pot,'" Henry offered.

"That is absolutely not the phrase I would have used, Henry Ryan." Mom threw him a look and then wrapped her arm around Chloe, urging her down the hall. She turned to talk to me over her shoulder. "I figured if you didn't see what was right in front of your face, maybe another man deserved a shot."

"Poor Joel never had a shot," Dad mumbled, surprising all of us and apparently even himself. He looked up, and then laughed. "Someone had to say it."

Climbing out of the car, I smiled at the memory of the rest of that evening: the ten minutes during which we'd all dissolved into hysterics over our shared experiences of getting food poisoning at inopportune times, the unbelievable crème brûlée my mother had served after dinner, and, much later, the way Chloe and I had barely made it back inside my house before falling into a tangle of limbs and sweat on my living room floor.

I turned the knob on my parents' front door, knowing my dad would still be up, but hoping not to wake my mother. The knob creaked and I eased it open with familiar care, lifting it slightly where I knew the wood swelled a little at the threshold.

But, to my surprise, Mom greeted me in the entryway, wearing her old purple robe and holding two cups of tea.

"I don't know why," she said, extending one cup to me, "but I was pretty sure you were going to turn up here tonight."

"Mother's intuition?" I asked, taking the cup and bending to kiss her cheek. I lingered there, hoping I could keep my emotions in check tonight.

"Something like that." Tears filled her eyes and she turned away before I could say something about them. "Come on, I know why you're here. I've got it down in the kitchen."

Five

"And you're sure we'll get the signatures on time?" I asked my assistant, who checked her watch and jotted something down in her notepad.

"Yes. Aaron's on his way over there now. We should have them back by lunch."

"Good," I said, closing the files and handing them back. "We'll give it a final look before the meeting and if everything goes—" The door to my outer office opened, and a very determined-looking Bennett walked inside. My assistant let out a terrified squeak and I waved for her to go. She practically sprinted out of there.

Long legs carried him across the room in only a few strides, and he stopped just on the other side of my desk, slapping two crisp white envelopes down on a stack of marketing reports.

I looked down to the envelopes and then back up to him. "Something about this is so familiar," I said. "Which one of us is going to slam the door and storm out to the stairwell?"

He rolled his eyes. "Just open them."

"Well, good morning to you, too, Mr. Ryan."

"Chloe, don't be a pain in the ass."

"You'd rather be a pain in mine?"

His eyes softened and he leaned over my desk to kiss me. He'd gotten home late last night, long after I'd fallen asleep. I'd woken to the sound of my alarm clock to find his warm and very naked body pressed against mine. I deserved some kind of a medal for managing to leave that bed.

"Good morning, Miss Mills," he said softly. "Now open the damn envelopes."

"If you insist. But don't say I didn't warn you. Slamming things down on desks has never really ended well for us. Well, for me. Maybe you could rectify that . . ."

"Chloe."

"Fine, fine." I lifted the flap on the one with my name and pulled a printed sheet of paper from inside. "ORD to CDG," I read. "Chicago to France." I looked up at him. "They're sending me somewhere?"

Bennett beamed, and frankly, he looked so good while doing it I was glad I was sitting down. "France. Marseille, to be exact. The second ticket is behind that one."

Plane tickets, one envelope for each of us. Scheduled to leave Friday. It was Tuesday already.

"I . . . I don't understand. We're going to France?

This isn't about last night, is it? Because we have busy lives, Bennett. These kinds of things will always happen. I promise I wasn't upset."

He rounded the desk and kneeled in front of me. "No. This isn't about last night. It's about a lot of nights. This is about me putting what's important first. And this," he said, motioning between us. "This is what's important. We hardly see each other anymore, Chloe, and that's not going to change after the move. I love you. I *miss* you."

"I miss you, too. But . . . ahhh, I'm a little surprised. France is . . . really far and there's so much to do and—"

"Not just France. A private house—a *villa*. It belongs to my friend Max, the one I went to school with? And it's beautiful and huge and *empty*," he added. "With a giant bed, *several* of them. A pool. We can cook and walk around naked; we don't even have to answer the phone if we don't want to. Come on, Chlo."

"I love that you threw in the walking-around-naked part," I said. "Because that's most definitely how you'd close the deal."

He moved closer, clearly aware my resolve was breaking. "I pride myself on always knowing my opponent, Miss Mills. So what do you say? Come with me? Please?"

"Jesus, Bennett. It's like ten in the morning and you're killing me with the swoons here."

"I debated tranquilizing you and throwing you over my shoulder, but that might make things sticky at customs."

I took a deep breath and peered down at the tickets. "Okay, so we'd leave on the ninth and come back . . . Wait, is this right?"

He followed my gaze. "What?"

"Three weeks? I can't just drop everything and go to France for *three weeks*, Bennett!"

He stood, confused. "Why? I was able to make arrangements and—"

"Are you serious? First, we're moving in a month. A month! And we haven't even picked out an apartment! Then there's my best friend, who was cheated on by the world's biggest asshat last week. And let's not forget the minor detail called *my job*? I have meetings and an entire department to hire and move to New York!"

His face fell; clearly this was not the reaction he'd anticipated. The sun was behind him and when he turned his head, tilting it the slightest bit, the light caught his eyelashes, the angles of his face.

Ugh. Guilt swelled in my chest like a balloon. "Fuck. I'm sorry." I leaned into him and laid my head against his shoulder. "That is absolutely not the way I meant to say all that."

Strong arms wrapped around me and I felt him exhale. "I know."

Bennett took my hand and led me to the small table in the corner of the room. He motioned for me to take a seat, while he took the chair opposite me. "Shall we negotiate?" he said, a challenge in his eyes I hadn't seen since he'd stepped into my office.

This I could do.

He leaned forward, hands clasped and elbows on the table in front of him. "The move," he began. "Admittedly, it's a big one. But we have a Realtor; I've seen the top three contenders. You just need to decide if you need to see them, or if you trust me to choose. We can let the Realtor handle the rest and pay people to do the actual packing and moving part." He raised a brow in question and I nodded for him to continue. "I know how much you care about Sara. Talk to her; see where she's at with all of this. You said you didn't even know if she was leaving him, right?"

"Yeah."

"So we'll cross that bridge when we come to it. And your job . . . I'm so incredibly proud of you, Chloe. I know how hard you work and how important you are. But there will never be a perfect time. We'll always be busy, there will always be people who want our attention, and there will always be things that feel like they can't wait. It's a good exercise for you in delegating tasks—I love you, but you suck at delegating. And it's going to be even more hectic when we move. When's the next time we'll have a chance to do this? I want to be with you. I want to speak French to you and make you come on a bed in France where nobody can just drop by on the weekend or call either of us away for work."

"You're making it very hard to be the responsible adult here," I said.

"Being responsible is overrated."

I felt my mouth fall open and could do nothing but gape at him. I was just about to ask who this easygoing person was, and what they'd done with my boyfriend, when there was a knock at the door. I pulled my eyes away from a very pleased boyfriend to see a terrified intern walk in, staring at Bennett with fear in her eyes. No doubt she'd drawn the short straw and been sent down to retrieve the Bastard.

"Um . . . Excuse me, Miss Mills," she stuttered, gaze locked on me instead of her real target. "They're waiting for Mr. Ryan in the conference room on twelve . . ."

"Thank you," I answered. She left and I turned back to Bennett.

"We'll discuss this later?" he asked quietly, standing. I nodded, still a little off balance from his change in attitude. "Thank you," I said, vaguely motioning to the tickets, but meaning so much more.

He kissed my forehead. "Later."

Travel had . . . never really worked out for Bennett and me. San Diego had been perfect while we were still tucked away in our own little bubble. It was when we tried to rejoin the living that it had all gone to hell. In a big way.

And then we'd planned to travel last Thanksgiving, and ended up canceling the trip because of work. We tried again in December; Bennett had been drowning in a huge fitness account that was set to launch just before the New Year, and we both had the Papadakis launch in early January. Somehow, though, I'd convinced him to come home with me for a long weekend over the holidays.

To meet my father.

Bennett hadn't wanted to—he'd been in the final stages of this huge campaign, had a family of his own to contend with. And a girlfriend who had spent the better part of the last year telling her father what a giant, overbearing dick her boss was, only to then finally admit she was having sex with this boss. This trip had disaster written all over it.

Bennett had been quiet throughout most of the flight,

and when he hadn't suggested we join the Mile High Club even once, I knew something was going on.

"You're being awfully respectful over there, Ryan. What's up?" I asked after we'd landed and were making our way to the rental car.

"What's that supposed to mean?"

"Well, you haven't made one inappropriate comment or referred to me riding, sucking, licking, touching, strok-ing, grabbing, or otherwise praising your dick once in the last three hours. I can practically hear you thinking and frankly, I'm a little concerned."

He reached down and smacked my ass. "Better? Your tits look great in that sweater, by the way."

"Talk to me."

"I'm meeting your father," he said, pulling at his collar.

"And?"

"And he knows what an asshole I was." I cleared my throat and he glared at me. "Can be."

"Can be?"

"Chloe."

"It's all part of the Bennett Ryan charm everyone goes on about," I said, batting my lashes at him. "Since when did you apologize for that?"

He sighed. "Since we're going to see your father. And if he owns a calendar, he would have figured out that I was sleeping with you while we worked together."

"I had to face your family after all that, too. I'm sure

Mina told Henry about the Bathroom Incident, and if Henry knows then Elliott knows. And if Elliott knows . . . oh my God, your mother knows we had sex in her favorite bathroom . . . when Joel was there on a blind setup to meet me." I smacked my palm to my forehead.

"Yeah, well, my family practically walks around wearing Team Chloe shirts under their regular clothes so it's a little different."

We reached the door to the rental agency and I took his hand, stopping him. "Look, my dad knows who his daughter is. He knows I can be a little spirited—"

"Ha!"

It was my turn to glare. "And he knows I give as good as I get. You're fine."

He sighed and leaned forward to rest his forehead against mine. "If you say so.

Dad let out an evil whistle as he circled the shiny black Benz now parked in his driveway, boots crunching in the snow. "Always figured there was only one reason a man would drive a car like this: compensating for something. Wouldn't you agree, Benson?"

"Bennett," he corrected under his breath, before smiling tightly over to me.

"It's Christmas, Dad. All the four-wheel-drive vehicles were gone."

Things didn't improve at dinner, either.

As we sat around the table, my father stared at Bennett like he was trying to match him up with a face he'd seen on the news. "Bennett, huh?" *he said, shooting a skeptical eye over his wineglass.* "What kind of a name is that?"

I groaned. "Daddy."

"My mother was a bit of a Jane Austen fan, sir. My brother's middle name is Willoughby so I like to think I got off easy."

Dad didn't even crack a smile at that. "Named after a character in a romance novel? I guess that explains a few things."

"Your first name, Frederick," *Bennett said, with a small smile.* "It's a good name, if you don't mind me saying so. Frederick Wentworth is also the hardworking, self-made protagonist in* Persuasion. *My mother made me read all of Austen's novels when I was in high school, and I generally do what my mother tells me."* He took a bite of his dinner, chewed, and swallowed before saying, "That advice also includes dating your daughter."

"Hmmm. Well, be careful with her," *Dad said, glaring at Bennett from across the table.* "My hygienist's boyfriend is in the mob, and I doubt anyone would miss you."

"Dad!"

He looked at me, eyes wide and innocent. "What?"

"Mark's boyfriend is not in the mob."

"*Of course he is. He's Italian.*"

"*That doesn't mean anything!*"

"*Trust me. I've met him. Drives a black car with very dark windows. Mark called him Fat Don at the office party.*"

"*His name is Glen, Dad, and he's studying to be a CPA. He's not in the mob.*"

"*I don't know why you have to be so damn argumentative all the time, Chloe. God only knows where you get it.*"

At that point Bennett started laughing so hard he had to excuse himself from the table.

Later, after Bennett won my father over by letting Dad beat him at Monopoly—how anyone would believe Bennett Ryan lost a game involving money, I'll never know—he snuck in from the guest room and climbed into my bed.

"*You're going to get us busted,*" *I said, already climbing on top of him.*

"*Not if you're quiet.*"

"*Hmm, I don't know. Can't tell you how many times my dad busted me for sneaking out when I was in high school, and I was very quiet.*"

"*Can we not talk about your dad right now? It's seriously distracting me from how hot it's going to be to fuck you in your teenage bed. And Jesus, Chloe. Are these even considered underwear?*" *he said, twisting his hands in the tiny straps of my panties and pulling. Hard.*

"Oh my God!" I whisper-shouted. "Those were new and—"

"You loved it," he finished, grinning. "Just doing my part to uphold tradition."

I wanted to argue but 1) he was right and 2) I was distracted as Bennett slid the torn fabric to the side and slipped a finger inside of me. He took my hip in his other hand, encouraging me to move over him.

"Like that," he said, lips parted and eyes trained between my legs. "Fuck—take your shirt off."

Ripped panties forgotten, I nodded, lifting my T-shirt over my head and tossing it behind us. He slipped in a second finger and I sped up, the bed frame squeaking softly beneath us.

Bennett sat, whispering "Shh," against my mouth. "Sit up a little."

I shifted onto my knees and watched as he pushed his pajama bottoms down his hips.

"Are we really doing this here?" I whispered. The bed was too small, the room too hot and too quiet—and my dad was just two doors down. It was stupid and inconvenient and I couldn't remember wanting something more.

I switched on the small lamp so I could see him better. His lips were swollen, his hair a mess, and his grin was totally ridiculous when he said, "I fucking love you, you filthy fucking girl. You want me to watch?"

"Yeah."

"Touch yourself," he whispered.

I did, way too slowly to get me anywhere, but the perfect speed to make his eyes grow to the size of saucers before he stretched to kiss me. He mumbled something against my lips, his tongue moving lazily against mine. He was all soft noises and hands everywhere, his cock sliding over my clit before finally pressing slowly into me.

It was a blur then, the feeling of being so full, of warm breath and warmer skin. Bennett sucked on my nipple, teeth dragging while I slid over him. I was so lost to everything else that I didn't even notice the familiar squeak of the hinge on my bedroom door.

"Oh for the love of Pete!" my dad yelled, and suddenly it was legs and arms and blankets being tossed everywhere. I heard the distant flailing of my father as he rushed back down the hall, muttering about his little girl and sex in his house and telltale signs of a heart attack.

Let's just say that neither Bennett nor I had ever been so grateful for anything as we were for the NDSU football player who needed an emergency root canal the next morning and whose coach, an old friend of my father's, insisted that only Dad could handle it. Dad was at the office, waiting on their arrival from Fargo before the sun was even up.

No, vacations never really seemed to work out for us.

Guilt ate away at me the rest of the morning. I shouldn't have been so hasty to tell Bennett it was impossible. Here he was, trying to be flexible, and I was the one telling him to consider work. What the hell was wrong with me? I tried to catch him between meetings. I tried to meet up with him for lunch. The closest I got was passing him in the hall, a group of executives babbling around him like fanboys around a celebrity.

"I need to talk to you," I mouthed.

"Bat signal?" I *think* he said back.

I shook my head. "Dinner?"

He nodded, blew me a kiss behind everyone's back, and was off, herded down the hall and into the elevator.

"So how are things?"

Sara shrugged, dragging another fry through ketchup before popping it into her mouth, but definitely not looking at me. "Things are fine."

I glared at her. Things were always *fine* with Sara.

"I'm serious!" she insisted, leaning back in her chair. "There's so much noise about it all. I'm just trying to figure out what is truth, and what isn't."

"Sounds like a good plan," I said.

"I've known him for so long it's just hard to reconcile it all. But, honestly, I'm doing fine."

"Sara, pardon the intrusion, because I suppose technically it's none of my business, but that is the biggest load of shit I've ever heard."

"What?"

"You heard me! This thing with Andy is a huge deal! Bennett wants us to go to France and besides the obvious twelve hundred fifty-four reasons why I shouldn't go, near the top of that list is you!"

"What?" she repeated, though a bit louder this time. "Bennett wants you to go to France! Oh my God that's amazing! And wait, what do you mean 'me'?"

"Yeah, he wants us to have some time away to reconnect before the craziness of New York is upon us all," I said, before balling up my napkin and throwing it at her. "And I hesitate to leave for three weeks because I'm worried about you!"

Sara laughed, standing to walk around the table and hug me. "That is the sweetest, most idiotic thing anyone has ever said to me. I love you, Chloe."

"But I'm moving," I added, squeezing her tightly. "These were going to be our last three weeks together."

Sara took the seat next to me. "I'm a big girl, and there are planes. I love—*love*—that you wanted to stay here and take care of me. But . . . I think Bennett might be right," she said, wincing a little. "You guys need this, and if you can make it work, well, you should throw some skimpy clothes in a bag and drag that man to France."

I laughed, leaning on her shoulder. "God, it would complicate things so much. I'd have to find someone to do interviews, sit in on all my meetings—"

"But would it be worth it?"

I smiled, remembering how excited Bennett had been when he'd told me about the trip, and how his face had fallen when I hadn't shared his enthusiasm. "Yeah, it would."

Six

I rolled over, grabbing my phone from the bedside table and muting the alarm with a swipe of my thumb. I was exhausted, having fallen asleep only two hours before. I'd worked until almost two and then tried to slip into bed without waking Chloe, but she'd stirred and climbed on top of me before I could say anything.

As if I would have stopped her.

I couldn't really complain that it meant another hour of sleep lost, but now, when her hand reached blindly beneath the blankets, sweeping down my stomach to curl around my cock, I knew I had to stop her. I had a flight to catch, alone.

She *was* coming to France, but she was leaving a day after me, insisting with a stubbornness all her own that she needed the rest of Friday to get the last few things sorted. I would have waited for her, but because the flights were all last minute there weren't any direct flights, nor were there any seats together anyway. Deciding to keep my flight, I figured I'd get there early and get us situated at Max's place.

"I don't think we have time," I mumbled into her hair.

"Not buying it," she said, voice croaky with sleep. "This guy," she said, squeezing my erection in her grip, "thinks we have plenty of time."

"The car is picking me up in fifteen minutes, and thanks to your appetite last night, I need another shower."

"There was that one time you only needed two minutes to come. You're telling me you don't have two minutes?"

"Morning sex is never only two minutes," I reminded her. "Not when you're all sleepy and rumpled and warm." I rolled out of bed and walked into my bathroom to the sound of her groan muffled by my stolen pillow.

When I emerged, clean and dressed, she sat up in bed, still hugging my pillow and sort-of-pretending she wasn't upset that we had to fly separately to France.

"Don't pout," I murmured, bending to kiss the corner of her mouth. "You'll just confirm what I've always suspected: you can't function without me."

I expected her to roll her eyes or pinch me playfully but she blinked down to my tie and reached to needlessly adjust it. "I *can* function without you. But I don't like being away from you. It feels like you take my home with you when you go."

Well, fuck.

I laid my garment bag across the bed and took her face in my hands until she looked up, and could see the effect her words had on me. She smiled, tongue slipping out to wet her lips.

With one final kiss, I whispered, "I'll see you in France."

———

I would lose a day in transit, arriving on Saturday. Chloe's flight was only twelve hours after mine, but because she couldn't go direct she had to red-eye it to New York and then leave for Paris the following day, getting into Marseille on Monday. It would give me time to prepare for her arrival, but, knowing Max, the house would be spotless and stocked with food and drink and I would have nothing to do.

An idle Bennett . . . and all that.

I settled into the first class cabin, declining the champagne, and pulled out my phone to text Chloe.

Boarded. See you across the pond.

My phone buzzed several seconds later. Rethinking this whole trip. There's a shoe sale at Dillons this weekend.

I laughed, choosing to ignore this one and slipping my phone back into my jacket pocket. Closing my eyes as the other passengers filed in past me, I remembered our past trips. We'd only traveled together a handful of times, but nothing ever went according to plan. Had I incurred some sort of vacation voodoo I wasn't aware of? It seemed we were destined to be plagued by trips that went terribly off course, were taken separately, were colored by miserable arguments . . . or were canceled altogether.

My stomach turned when I remembered our attempt at a vacation last Thanksgiving. On impulse one weekend we'd purchased tickets to St. Bart's and rented a house on the water. It was meant to be perfect but instead it led to the first time Chloe stopped speaking to me since our reconciliation.

———

"Motherfucking cocksucking son of a whore."

I looked up from my desk, my eyebrows inching to my hairline as Chloe slammed my door and stormed to my desk.

"Did the gimp escape the dungeon again, Miss Mills?"

"Close enough. Papadakis is pushing up launch."

I stood so abruptly my chair skidded back and banged into the wall. "What?"

"January is the new March, apparently. The first press blast is set to go out January seventh."

"That's a horrible time to pitch something like this! Everyone is still drunk or cleaning up the holiday mess. No one is buying fancy apartments."

"That's what I told Big George."

"Did you also tell him he needs to stick to counting his Benjamins and leave the marketing to us?"

She laughed, crossing her arms across her chest. "I may have actually used those words. With a few other gangster terms thrown in."

I sat back down, rubbing my hands over my face. Our flight was scheduled to leave in the morning, on Thanksgiving Day, and there was no way we could leave work now. "You told him this was okay?"

Across the desk, I could sense that she grew completely still. "What was my option?"

"To tell him we're not going to be ready!"

"But that's a lie. We can be ready."

I dropped my hands, gaping at her. "Yes, but only if we work fifteen-hour days through the holidays—and all to accommodate his shitty timing for a launch."

She threw her hands up, eyes on fire. "He's paying us a million dollars for basic marketing and we're inking a deal for another ten-million-dollar media campaign. You think fifteen-hour days are unreasonable to keep our biggest client?"

"Of course not! But he's also not your only client! Rule number one in business is to not ever let the big dog know how small the other dogs are."

"Damnit, Bennett. I'm not going to tell him we can't deliver."

"Sometimes a little pushback is a good thing. You're being green, Mills. If you weren't sure, you should have sent the call to me."

I immediately wanted to pull the words back into my mouth. Her eyes went wide, her mouth dropped, and fuck, her hands curled into fists at her sides. I reached down to cover my balls.

"Are you fucking serious right now? Are you going to cut my fucking steak at dinner, too, you egomaniacal asshat?"

I couldn't help myself. "Only if I can feed it to you and help you chew."

Her face smoothed and I could see her calculate how much effort she wanted to put into kicking my ass. "We're skipping St. Bart's," she said, flatly.

"Obviously. Why do you think I'm pissed?"

"Well, even if we did still go at this point, you'd be sleeping alone with your hand and a tube of lube."

"I could work with that. These two hands provide some variety."

She blinked away, jaw clenched. "Are you trying to make me more angry?"

"Sure, why not."

Dark eyes turned back on me, narrowed. Her voice shook a little with one word: "Why?"

"So you can feel the pain more. Because you should have told George that these kinds of decisions have to be cleared with the entire team and we'd have an answer for him after the holiday."

"How do you know I didn't say that?"

"Because you came in here and delivered news. You didn't act like it was a suggestion."

She stared at me, eyes flashing through a hundred responses. I waited to see how many curse words she could string together but she surprised me instead, and turned to leave my office.

———

Chloe didn't stay over that night. It was only the second night we'd spent apart after her presentation at J. T. Miller last June, and I didn't even try to sleep. Instead, I watched Mad Men on Netflix and wondered which of us would apologize first.

The problem was I was right, and I knew it.

Thanksgiving morning arrived with snow flurries and a wind so strong it pushed me forward into the building as I walked, alone, from the parking garage to my office.

It had never occurred to me that she would leave me again after our fight. I suspected Chloe and I were in it for the long haul, whether the long haul officially began tomorrow or ten years in the future. There wasn't anything she could do to scare me off.

And while I felt the same was true for her, she rarely walked away from a fight. She either battled with me until I was figuratively on my knees or she ended up on her knees in an entirely different way.

Only a few RMG employees were at work on Thanksgiving—the members of the Papadakis team. And every one of them glared at Chloe as she walked down the hall to get some coffee. Knowing her, she had probably worked late last night and slept under her desk.

*She didn't even glance over to where I stood in the door-
way to the conference room. Still, I could almost hear her
thinking as she passed every disgruntled team member: "You
can suck my dick. And you, too, can suck my dick. And you?
The slacker with the pathetic pout? You can really suck my
dick."*

*She headed to her office, settled in, and left her door
open.*

Come and get me, *she was saying.* Come on in and let's
have it out.

*But for as much as everyone probably wanted to give her
an earful for making us cancel our holiday plans, no one did.
Each of us had been raised in the business world under the
same ethos: work trumps all. The last person to leave work is
the hero. The first person in has bragging rights. Working over
holidays gets you into heaven.*

*And while a more experienced executive would have told
Papadakis that what he'd asked wasn't possible, as always I
admired Chloe's determination. This wasn't just about meeting a new milestone for her. This was her launching her career. This was her foundation. Chloe was me a few years ago.*

———

*After everyone else had left for the evening, I knocked on her
open door, gently alerting her to my presence.*

*"Mr. Ryan," she said, pulling off her glasses and looking
up at me. The city skyline winked behind her, speckled lights*

covering her entire wall of windows. "Here to show me how to grow a penis so I can get the job done?"

"Chloe, I'm pretty sure if you wanted to grow one, you could do it by will alone."

She let a half smile form, pushing back from her desk and crossing her legs. "I'd grow one just so I could ask you to suck on it."

I couldn't contain my laughter, bending over and collapsing into the chair across the desk from her. "I knew you were going to say that."

Her eyebrows pulled together a little. "Well, before you say anything else, yes, I know this sucks. And . . . I think you were right. We could be in St. Bart's right now, on the beach."

I started to speak, but she held up her hand to urge me to wait.

"But the thing is, Bennett, no matter how much I should have, I didn't want to tell Papadakis no. I wanted to deliver, because we can, and we should. It's down to the wire anyway and we've had a lot of time to work on this. It felt disingenuous to say we couldn't make it happen."

"True," I conceded, "but by letting him push a milestone ahead to the beginning of the quarter, you've set a precedent."

"I know," she said, rubbing her temples with her fingertips.

"But actually, I wasn't coming in here to tell you what you'd done was wrong. I was coming in here to tell you I understand why you did it. I can't really fault you."

She dropped her hands, eyeing me cautiously.

"At this point in your career, I can't be surprised you said yes to Papadakis."

Her mouth opened and I could see a litany of curse words form on her tongue.

"Easy, firecracker," I said, leaning forward and holding up my hands. "I don't mean you're naïve; I'm not pulling the 'seasoning' card again—though it's true no matter how much you hate to hear it. I mean you're still building. You want to show the world that you're Atlas—and to a Titan, that fucking celestial sphere weighs nothing. It's just that it's impacted the entire team, and over a holiday. I get why you did it, and I also get why you're conflicted. I'm sorry this is hard for you, because I've been there." I lowered my voice, moved a little closer. "It sucks."

The room seemed to grow darker, the sun dipping behind the horizon just as I'd finished my sentence. Chloe watched me, face smooth and practically unreadable.

Well, unreadable to anyone else. Anyone who hadn't seen that face a thousand times, the one that told me she wanted to smack me, kiss me, scratch me, and then fuck me.

"Don't smirk," she said, eyes narrowing. "I see what you're doing."

"What am I doing?"

"Trying to build me up. Being a hardass, yet also my lover. Damnit, Bennett."

"You're going to fuck me in your office!" I crowed, my words colored with surprise and glee. "God, you're easy."

98

She stood quickly, walking around the desk and reaching immediately for my tie. "Damnit." She unknotted it, wrapping it around my eyes and tying it behind my head. "Stop studying me," she hissed into my ear. "Stop seeing everything."

"Never." I closed my eyes behind the silk fabric and let my other senses take over, inhaling the delicate citrus scent of her perfume, reaching to feel the soft skin of her forearms. I moved my hands slowly down her body and turned her around, pulling her back to my chest. "This better?"

Her quiet huff wasn't for my benefit; it was a sound of genuine frustration. "Bennett," she murmured, leaning back. "You're making me crazy."

I gripped her hips, pulling her to me so she could feel the hard line of my cock against her ass. "At least some things never change."

———

I blinked up to the flight attendant, who bent low to catch my eye and had obviously just said something.

"I'm sorry?" I asked.

"Would you like a beverage with your meal?"

"Ah, yes," I said, pulling my brain from the memory of Chloe's body, tight and coiled around me as I'd fucked her over her desk. "Just some Grey Goose and a cup of ice, please."

"And for lunch? We have filet mignon or a cheese and olive plate."

I ordered the latter and glanced out the window. From thirty thousand feet up, I could be anywhere. But I had the distinct feeling I was headed back in time.

I hadn't been back to France since my return to the States, when I met Chloe in person. For what felt like the hundredth time, I registered how that old Bennett didn't feel familiar in the slightest.

Thanksgiving had been a revelation in part because, before Chloe, I would have also said yes to George's demand without even a thought. Chloe was so similar to me in so many ways, it was actually a little frightening.

I smiled as I thought back to my mother's advice:

"Find a woman who will be your equal in every way. Don't let yourself fall for someone who'll put your world before theirs. Fall for the powerhouse who lives as fearlessly as you do. Find the woman who makes you want to be a better man."

Well, I had found her. Now all I had to do was wait for her to get here, so I could make sure she knew.

―――――

The path leading to our borrowed villa was covered in small, smooth stones. They were brown and uniform in size, and although they were clearly selected for their appearance and how well they fit the landscaping, it was refreshingly obvious that the grounds were meant to be enjoyed, not treated as a precious museum piece. Flower beds and urns lined both sides of the path, each spilling over with bright, colorful blossoms. There were trees everywhere, and off in the distance was a little seating area, screened from the rest of the yard by a wall of blooming vines.

Truly, I had never seen a more beautiful country home. The house was a soft red, the color of faded clay, and weathered to an absolutely gorgeous effect. White shutters framed the tall windows on the first and second floors, and more vibrant flowers lined beds against the doors. The perfume in the air was a mixture of ocean and peony.

Bougainvillea crawled up a trellis and framed the French provincial-inspired narrow double doorway. The top step was cracked, but swept clean, and a simple, soft green mat lay atop the sun-bleached concrete.

I turned, looking behind me at the yard. In the far corner and beneath several fig trees, a long table was covered in a brilliant orange tablecloth, the tabletop decorated simply with a narrow line of tiny blue bottles of different shapes and sizes. Clean white plates were spaced at even intervals, waiting for a dinner party to appear. A green lawn stretched to where I stood on the narrow porch, broken only by the occasional inground planter bursting with purple, yellow, and pink flowers.

I pulled the key from my pocket and entered the house. From the outside, it was clearly large, but it almost seemed to expand like an optical illusion inside.

Christ, Max, this seems a little excessive. I knew his house in the Provence region was large, but I didn't realize there were so many fucking *rooms*. Just from the front door, I could see at least a dozen doorways connecting off the main hall, and doubtless there were countless other rooms upstairs and out of sight.

I paused in the entryway, staring at the enormous urn that looked like the larger cousin to a small vase my mother had in her dining room hutch; the cerulean blue base glaze was identical, and the same beautiful yellow lines bled down its curved sides. I remembered the gift from when Max brought it for my mother the first time he'd come home with me, over the winter holidays. I hadn't realized at the time how personal the hostess gift had been to him, but now, looking around his vacation home, I could see the same artist's work everywhere: in plates mounted above the mantel, in a hand-made teapot and a set of simple cups on a tray in the parlor.

I smiled, reaching out to touch the urn. Chloe would completely lose it when she saw it; it was her favorite thing in my mother's house. A feeling overcame me that we were almost fated to have come here.

After her birthday dinner in January, Chloe hesitated in the dining room, glancing at Mom's impressive art collection in the hutch. But instead of going for the obvious gleam of the Tiffany vases or the intricate detail of the carved wooden bowls, she went straight for a tiny blue vase in the corner.

"I don't think I've ever seen this color before," she said, awestruck. "I didn't think this color existed outside of the imagination."

Mom walked over, pulled it from the shelf. Under the soft light of the chandelier, the color seemed to almost wink and change even as Chloe held it still in her hand. I'd never noticed before how pretty the piece was.

"It's one of my favorites," Mom admitted, smiling. "I've never seen anything this color anywhere else either."

But that wasn't entirely true, I thought, as I stepped away from the urn and walked to the mantel. The ocean here was that color, when the sun was high over the horizon and the sky was clear. Only then did it hit that exact same blue, like the heart of the deepest sapphire. An artist who lived here would know that.

On the shelf were three handmade *santon*s, the small nativity figurines traditionally made by artists in Provence. All were obviously made by the same artist who made Mom's vase, the giant urn, and the rest of the art here. He or she must have been local, whether still alive or not, but perhaps Chloe would have the opportunity to see some other pieces while visiting. The coincidence, the perfection of it, felt almost surreal.

The blues and greens of the platter mounted over the mantel caught the late afternoon sun and redirected the light, casting the wall behind it in a soft blue glow. With the wind blowing through the trees outside and the sunlight winking in and out of shadows, the effect was a bit like watching the surface of the ocean move in the wind. Combined with the crisp white furniture and otherwise simple decorating in the sitting room, it immediately made me feel calmer. The world of RMG and Papadakis, of work and stress and the constant buzzing of my phone, felt a million miles away.

Unfortunately, so did Chloe.

As if she could hear my thoughts from where she sat on a plane headed over the Atlantic, my phone buzzed in my pocket and her unique text chime rang out in the silent room.

Pulling my phone from my pocket, I glanced down and read the message: Mechanic strike. All flights canceled. I'm stuck in New York.

Seven

"What do you mean *grounded*?" I said, gaping at the woman on the other side of the counter. She was about my age, with freckled cheeks and strawberry-blond hair pulled back into a sleek ponytail. She also looked like she was two seconds from strangling me and every other person in the international terminal at LaGuardia.

"Unfortunately we've just been informed of a mechanic union strike," she said flatly. "All Provence Airlines flights in and out of the airport have been canceled. We're terribly sorry for the inconvenience."

Well, she didn't sound very sorry. I continued to stare, blinking rapidly as her words sunk in. "Excuse me, *what*?"

She arranged her features into a tight, practiced smile. "All flights have been canceled due to the strike." I glanced over her shoulder to the Provence Airlines departure and arrival screens. Sure enough, CANCELED was emblazoned across each line.

"You're telling me I'm stuck here? Why didn't any-one tell me this in Chicago?"

"We'd be happy to help you make accommodations for the night—"

"No no no, that's impossible. Please, check again."

"Ma'am, as I told you, there are no Provence Air-lines flights taking off or landing. You can check with the other airlines to see if they can accommodate you. There's nothing else I can do."

I groaned, letting my forehead fall to the counter. Bennett was waiting for me, probably sitting outside in the sun at this very moment, laptop open and working like the overachieving loser he was. *God, he turns me on.*

"This can't be happening," I said, straightening and giving the attendant the most pleading expression I could muster. "The sweetest jackass in the world is waiting for me in France and I can't screw this up!"

"Mkaaaay," she said clearing her throat and straight-ening a stack of papers.

I was doomed. "How long?" I asked.

"There's no way to tell. Obviously they'll try and re-solve the issue as soon as possible, but it could be one day, it could be more."

Well, that was helpful.

With a dramatic sigh and a few muffled swear words I dragged myself from the counter, in search of a quiet corner to call my assistant. Oh, and to text Bennett. This was not going to go over well.

The phone rang within seconds.

I maneuvered through the crowd, through the throngs of stranded passengers taking up virtually every flat surface in the Provence Airlines terminal, and stopped at a tiny alcove near the restrooms.

"Hi."

"What the fuck do you mean 'stuck in New York'?!" he shouted.

I winced, pulling the phone from my ear before taking a much-needed calming breath.

"It means exactly what you think it means. We've been grounded, no flights in or out. I'm having a few people check with Delta and a few other airlines, but I'm sure everyone else has already done that, too."

"This is unacceptable!" he roared. "Do they know who you are? Let me talk to someone."

I laughed. "Nobody here knows or cares who I am. Or you for that matter."

He was silent for a moment, long enough that I actually looked to see if I'd dropped the call. I hadn't. The sound of birds singing filled the line, a wind chime off in the distance. When he finally did speak, it was in that low, steady voice I'd become so accustomed to.

The one that still sent goose bumps along my skin. The one he used when he meant business.

"Tell them to get your ass on a plane," he said, enunciating every word.

"Everything is overbooked on *every* plane, Bennett. What the hell do you want me to do? Catch a ride on a boat? Use a portkey? Simmer down, I'll get there as soon as I can."

He groaned, and I could tell the moment he realized he couldn't argue or charm his way out of this. "But when?"

"I don't know, babe. Tomorrow, maybe? The next day? Soon, I promise."

With a resigned sigh he asked, "So what now?" I heard the sound of a door opening and closing, the tinkle of soft music in the background.

"We wait." I sighed. "I'll get a room, maybe get some work done. Maybe I can check out those apartments while I'm here. And then I promise, the first available flight out of here? I'm on it. Even if I have to take out a few businessmen with the heel of my shoe—I'll get there."

"You bet your ass you will," he said.

I shook my head to clear it from the sound of his commanding voice. "So tell me about the house. Is it as gorgeous as I imagine?"

"Better. I mean, your company would obviously improve it, but damn. Max really outdid himself on this one."

"Well, try and enjoy it. Sit in the sun, swim, read something trashy. Walk around barefoot."

"Walk around barefoot? That's an unusual request, even for you."

"Humor me."

"Yes, ma'am."

I grinned. "Damn, I think I like this side of you. Pretty sexy when you take orders, Ryan."

He laughed softly into the phone. "Oh, and Chloe?"

"Hmm?"

"I hope you didn't pack any panties. You won't be needing them."

I spent the rest of the day at the airport, praying for a miracle or a flight to France. I got neither.

It took hours to locate my luggage, so by the time I finally walked through the door of my hotel room, I was ready to pass out. With the time difference it was too late, or too early, to call Bennett, so I'd sent him a short text while I ran myself a bath and ordered a bottle of wine, along with anything containing chocolate, from the room service menu.

I'd just climbed into the large tub—wineglass and chocolate cheesecake balanced precariously on the edge—when my phone rang. My hand fumbled around

Christina Lauren

on the tile floor until I found it, and a smile filled me when Bennett's face lit up the screen.

"I thought you'd be asleep," I said.

"Bed's too big."

I smiled at his sleepy voice. This was the Bennett who would roll over in the middle of the night, limbs warm and heavy, sweet words mumbled into my skin. He'd always been so much *better* at all of this than I had, even from the beginning.

"What are you doing?" he asked, bringing my attention back to the phone.

"Bubble bath," I said, and grinned at the sound of his groan on the other end of the line.

"No fair."

"What about you?"

"Just going over some paperwork."

"Did you find my note?

"Note?"

"I left you something."

"You did?"

"Mm-hmm. Check your laptop bag."

I heard the creak of leather as he stood, the sound of feet padding across a tile floor followed by laughter. "Chloe," he said, laughing harder now. "It looks like someone slipped a ransom note in here."

"Very funny."

"'Three observations about today: I didn't get everything done on my to-do list, the salad you made me for lunch was delicious, and, most importantly, I love you,'" he read, and then fell silent as he read the rest of the note to himself. When he finished, he grumbled, "I . . . *fuck*. It makes me insane that you aren't here."

I closed my eyes. "The universe is conspiring against us."

"You know, there's a part of me that wants to say none of this would have happened if you weren't so stubborn, and would have just come with me in the first place." I started to protest. "*But*," he said, continuing, "your determination is one of the things I love most about you. You never settle. You'd never expect someone to do a job you wouldn't do yourself. And you wouldn't be the woman I fell in love with if you changed that. It's exactly what I would have done. As usual. And also a little creepy to realize how alike we are."

I sat up in the cooling water, bringing my knees to my chest. "Thank you, Bennett. That means a lot to me."

"Well, I meant it. And you can show me your appreciation when you get that hot little ass to France. Deal?"

I rolled my eyes. "Deal."

I didn't get to France the next day. Or the day after that. And by day three I was actually trying to remember why hitching a ride on a boat had seemed like such a bad idea in the first place.

It's possible I called Bennett more in those three days than in the entirety of our relationship, but it wasn't enough, and did nothing to ease the hollow ache that had taken up permanent residence inside my chest.

I kept myself busy, but there was no denying I was homesick. I wasn't sure exactly when it had happened, but at some point, Bennett had become it for me. As in *it* it. The One.

And it was fucking terrifying.

I'd come to this realization while out for a walk. My assistant had called, saying she'd been able to get me on an Air France flight later that night. My first thought had been of Bennett, and how I couldn't wait to tell him I was on my way. I'd nearly sprinted to my hotel room.

But then I'd stopped, heart racing and lungs on fire. When had this happened, when had he become my everything? And I wondered, was it possible he was trying to tell me he felt the same way? I packed in a daze, throwing clothes aimlessly into my bag and collecting my things around the room. I thought back on how much he'd changed in the last year. The quiet moments at night, the way he looked at me sometimes as if I were the only woman on the planet. I wanted to be with him—always. And not just in the same apartment or bed, but for good.

It was then that I was struck by an idea so crazy, so insane, that I literally burst out laughing. I'd never been the type of woman to sit back and wait for the things I wanted to appear, so why should this be any different? And that was it.

Bennett Ryan had no idea what was about to hit him.

Eight

As impossible as it seemed, I was bored out of my fucking mind in this beautiful, enormous French villa. The place required no cleaning or handyman work, my VPN connection was so slow I couldn't get on the RMG server to conduct actual business, and—perhaps most strangely—I felt like there were certain things I shouldn't do until Chloe got here.

It felt wrong to dive into the infinity pool knowing she was stuck in New York. I didn't want to walk through the vineyards bordering the house, because it seemed like something we should discover at the same time. Max's housekeeper had put out some bottles of wine for us to enjoy, but surely only a giant asshole would drink them alone. My claim to this house was hers, too. I'd still only opened one bedroom door, and slept there, not wanting to go through our options until she'd arrived. Together we would pick out where we would spend our nights.

Of course, if I said any of this to her she would laugh at me and tell me I was being dramatic. But that's why I wanted her here. Something monumental happened to me the other day when I used the bat signal, and that sense of urgency hadn't diminished, and probably wouldn't until she was here and had heard what I had to say.

I walked through the gardens, stared out at the ocean in the distance, and checked my phone again, reading Chloe's most recent text for the hundredth time:

Looks like Air France might have an open seat.

She'd sent this one three hours ago. Although it seemed promising, her previous three texts had been similar, and ultimately she'd been bumped from those flights. Even if she had left three hours ago, she wouldn't make it to Marseille until tomorrow morning, at best.

Out of the corner of my eye, I saw a small figure emerge from the back of the house and place a platter of food on the table closest to the pool. Another peek at the clock on my phone told me that I'd managed to kill a few hours, and it was finally time for lunch. The house had come with a cook, a fifty-something woman named Dominique, who baked bread every morning, and, so far, served some variety of fish, fresh garden greens, and figs at lunch. Dessert was handmade *macarons* or tiny cookies with jam thumbprints. If Chloe didn't get here soon, Dominique would have to roll me to the door to greet my lady friend.

Beside my plate was a large glass of wine, and when I looked over at Dominique, she'd stopped at the threshold of the back door, pointed to the wine, and said, "Le boire. Vous vous ennuyez, et solitaire."

Well, shit. I *was* bored, and I *was* lonely. One glass of wine couldn't hurt. I wasn't celebrating—I was surviving, right? I thanked Dominique for lunch, and sat down at the table, trying to ignore the perfect breeze, the perfect temperature, the sound of the ocean not even a half mile in the distance, the feel of the warm tile beneath my bare feet. I wouldn't enjoy a single second until Chloe was here.

Bennett, you are one pathetic navel-gazer.

As usual, the fish was incredible, and the salad with tiny tart onions and little cubes of a sharp, white cheese packed so much flavor that before I knew it, my wineglass was empty and Dominique was at my side, quietly refilling it.

I began to stop her, telling her I needed no more wine. "Je vais bien, je n'ai pas besoin de plus."

She winked at me. "Puis l'ignorer."

Then ignore it.

———

One bottle of wine down and I began wondering why I hadn't bought a villa in France myself. I had lived in the country before, after all, and while the memories were bittersweet—time away from friends and family, a grueling work schedule—I'd lived here in a time of my life that felt so short in hindsight. I was still young. I was still starting out, really. Thank fuck Chloe and I had found each other when we still had our whole lives ahead of us.

Hell, if Max could find a gorgeous place like this, I could find one that was even more lush and beautiful.

The wine had left my limbs warm and heavy, my head full of rambling thoughts that seemed to have no reason. How insane would it have been to know Chloe in my early twenties? We would have torn this place up, and probably lasted only a weekend. Isn't it amazing how you meet the person you're meant to meet, when you're *supposed* to meet her?

I fumbled with my phone and texted Chloe: I'm so glad we met when we did. Even if you were an enormous pain in my ass you're still the best thing that ever hapened to me.

I stared intently at my phone, looking for an indication that she was replying, but nothing. Had her phone died? Or was she asleep in the hotel? Could she text on the airline? I did the mental calculation, knowing she was six hours? Seven hours behind . . . ? No, too complicated. I smiled at Dominique as she poured me another glass of wine, and I texted Chloe again: Not drinking all of the winembut what I have is dellicious! I promis to save some for you.

I stood, tripping over . . . something. I frowned down at the lawn and wondered if I'd stepped on a small animal. Discarding the thought, I walked into the garden, stretching my arms and letting out a long, happy sigh. I felt relaxed for the first time since I'd last fucked Chloe, which was about a zillion years ago. With a full stomach and a bit of wine in me, I realized I hadn't taken the time to plan for Chloe's arrival at all. We had some things to get out of the way first. We had some talking to do, some planning.

Would I lead her to the garden, pull her down onto the lawn with me, and make her listen? Or wait for a quiet moment over dinner and then go to her, guiding her out of the chair and close to me? I knew what I wanted to say—I'd gone over the words a million times in my head on the flights here—but I didn't know when I would say it.

Best to let her be here a few days before dropping the hammer.

I closed my eyes, leaned my head back, and tilted my head up to the sky. I let myself enjoy it for just a beat. The weather was spectacular. The last time I'd been outside in the sun with Chloe was at a barbecue at Henry's the previous weekend, and it had only been marginally warm. After a day in the sun and wind, we'd gone home and had some of the laziest, quietest sex I could remember.

I opened my eyes and immediately clapped a hand over my face in the bright sun. "Ow. *Fuck.*"

Dominique appeared several yards away and pointed to the front gate. "Allez," she said, telling me to go. "Se promener. Vous êtes ivre."

I laughed. Hell yes, I was tipsy. She'd poured the entire bottle of wine for me. "Je suis ivre parce que vous me versa une bouteille entière de vin." I think that's what I said.

With a smile, she lifted her chin. "Allez chercher des fleurs dans la rue. Demandez Mathilde."

———

This was good. I had a task. Find some flowers. Ask for Mathilde. I bent to tie my shoe and headed out of the property, toward town. Dominique was a wily one, getting me drunk and then sending me off on errands so I wasn't moping around the house all day. She and Chloe would get along swimmingly.

Not a half mile down the road, there was a small storefront with flowers spilling out of every conceivable container: vases and baskets, boxes and urns. Over the door was a small sign written in looping script that said simply, MATHILDE.

Bingo.

A bell rang as I entered, and a young blond woman stepped from the back into the small main room of the store.

Greeting me in French, she quickly gave me a once-over and then asked, "You're the American?"

"Oui, mais je parle français."

"But I also speak English," she said, her thick accent curling around each word. "And it is my store, so we'll practice for me."

She raised her brows flirtatiously, as if to challenge me. She was beautiful, no doubt, but her lingering eye contact and sexy smile made me a touch uneasy.

119

And then it hit me: Dominique knew I was bored and lonely, but she probably had no idea that I was waiting for Chloe's arrival. She'd filled me with wine and then sent me to the hot young single woman down the street.

Oh dear God.

Mathilde moved a little closer, adjusting some flowers in a tall, slim vase. "Dominique said you were staying at Mr. Stella's."

"You know Max?"

Her laugh was husky and quiet. "Yes, I know Max."

"Oh," I said, eyes widening. Of course. "You mean you *know* Max."

"This doesn't make me unique," she said, laughing again. Looking away from her flowers, she asked, "Are you here for flowers? Or do you think perhaps Dominique sent you for something else?"

"My girlfriend is coming tomorrow she was stuck in New York and then they had a strike and now she's coming," I blurted out in one steady, awkward word-flood.

"So you're here for flowers, then." Mathilde paused, looking around the store. "What a lucky woman she is. You are very handsome." Her eyes slid back to me. "Perhaps you'll be sober by then?"

I frowned. Straightening, I muttered, "I'm not *that* tipsy."

"No?" Her eyebrows lifted and an amused smile spread across her face. She moved back through the store, collecting an assortment of flowers as she walked. "You are charming anyway, Friend of Max. The wine just makes you less inhibited. I bet normally you button up your shirts and frown at people who will walk too slowly in front of you."

My frown deepened. That did sound a little like me. "I take my work seriously but I'm not like that . . . all the time."

She smiled, tying some twine around the flowers. Mathilde handed me the bouquet and winked. "You're not at work here. Keep your shirt unbuttoned. And don't sober up for your lover. There are nine beds in that house."

———

The front door was open. Had Dominique left and not closed it behind her? Panic seized me. What if something had happened when I was in town? What if the house had been ransacked? Despite Mathilde's advice, I sobered instantly.

But it hadn't been ransacked. It was exactly as I left it, with just a bit more wind blowing through the open door. Yet . . . I hadn't come out this way; I'd walked from the backyard to the front gardens.

Down the hall, I heard water running, and I called out to Dominique, "Merci pour l'idée, Dominique, mais ma co-pine arrive demain." She should know as soon as possible that I was spoken for. Who knows if she would start inviting women over here? Is that what she did for Max? *Dear God, the man hasn't changed one bit.*

As I neared the closest bedroom off the hall, I realized

that what I'd heard was a shower. And just inside the door were suitcases.

Chloe's suitcases.

———

I could have barreled in there and scared the ever-loving shit out of her. She had, after all, been stupid enough to leave the front door open enough for it to blow wide in the wind, and then climbed in the shower. I clenched my jaw and fists as I imagined what might have happened if someone else had decided to walk into the house instead of me.

Fuck. I hadn't seen her in days and I already wanted to strangle and then kiss the hell out of her. I felt a smile pull at my mouth. This was us. It was such a familiar battle of love and frustration, desire and exasperation. She would push every button I had, and then uncover new ones I didn't even know I had, and push those.

Her quiet singing drifted from the bathroom into the bedroom I'd claimed the first night here. As I moved closer, peeking around the doorway to where she stood, I was greeted by the sight of her long wet hair slick and shiny down her naked back. And then she bent over so her perfect ass was in the air as she shaved her legs, and kept singing to herself.

Part of me wanted to climb in, take the razor from her hand, and finish the job for her, kissing every smooth inch. Another part of me wanted to climb in and make good on the promise to take her from behind, slowly and carefully. But an even larger part of me relished playing the voyeur. She still didn't know I was there, and seeing her like this— thinking she was alone, singing quietly, maybe even thinking about me?—was like a cold glass of water on a scorching day. I would never get tired of watching her in any setting. And naked, wet, and in the shower wasn't too far from the top scenario on the list.

She rinsed her leg and stood, turning to clear the conditioner from her hair, and that's when she saw me. A smile exploded across her face, her nipples tightened, and in that moment I almost shattered the glass shower door to get to her.

"How long have you been standing there?"

I shrugged, looking down the length of her body.

"Such a creeper."

"*Still* a creeper, you mean." I moved a little closer, crossing my arms over my chest as I leaned against the wall. "When did you get here, you sneak?"

"About a half hour ago."

"I thought you just caught a plane in the States? Did you go by portkey after all?"

She laughed, tilting her head back under the showerhead for one final rinse, before turning off the water. "I caught the first one I told you about. I thought it would be fun to mislead and surprise you." Taking her long hair in both hands, she pulled it over her shoulder and squeezed the water from it, watching me with eyes that grew increasingly hungry. "I think I was hoping you'd come home to find me naked in the shower. May have been why I stepped *into* the shower."

"I'll admit it's pretty fucking convenient because I'm ready to be naked myself."

Chloe pushed open the door and came directly to me. "I wanted that pretty mouth on me as soon as I heard you were flirting with the flower girl."

I scowled. "Oh please." And then I paused. "How did you know about that?"

She smiled. "Dominique speaks very good English. Said she grew tired of your moping and sent you down there because you're so cute when you're annoyed. I agreed."

"She—*what?*"

"I'm glad you didn't decide to bring Mathilde back with you, though. That could have been awkward."

"Or it could have been awesome," I teased, pulling her against me and wrapping a towel from the rack around her shoulders. I felt the water from her breasts soak into my clothes.

She's here. She's here. She's here.

I bent, brushed my lips over hers. "Hey, sweetheart."

"Hey," she whispered, wrapping her arms around me. "Have you ever been with two women at once?" she asked, leaning back and running her hands up under my shirt as I worked to dry her off. "I can't believe I haven't ever asked you that."

"I missed you."

"I missed you, too. Answer my question."

I shivered. "Yes."

Her hands were cold and her nails felt sharp when she scratched down my torso. "More than two at a time?"

Shaking my head, I bent to run my nose along her jaw. She smelled like home, like my Chloe: her own mild citrus scent and the soft natural smell of her skin. "Weren't you saying something about wanting my mouth on you?"

"Specifically between my legs," she instructed.

"I assumed." I bent, scooped her up, and carried her to the bed.

When I put her down on the edge, she sat up, leaning back on her hands behind her, pulling her feet up on the edge of the bed . . . and spread her legs. She looked up at me, and whispered, "Take your clothes off."

Holy Christ this woman was going to kill me with views like that. I kicked my shoes across the room, yanked off my socks, and reached behind me to pull my shirt over my head. Giving her a few seconds to reacquaint herself with my bare chest, I scratched my stomach and gave her a smile. "See something you like?"

"Are we giving shows?" Her hand slipped over her thigh and between her legs. "I can do that."

"Are you fucking kidding me," I breathed, fumbling with my belt buckle and pulling the buttons of my jeans free in a single movement. I nearly fell over trying to get them off.

Her hand moved away, and then she reached both arms

out for me. "On top," she said quietly, apparently not wanting my mouth after all. "Over me, I want to feel your weight."

It was perfect, like this, without pretense. We both wanted to make love before we did anything else: looking around, eating, catching up.

Her skin was cool, and mine still felt flushed from the sun, my uphill walk back to the villa, and the thrill of seeing her here so unexpectedly. The contrast was astounding. Beneath me she was nothing but smooth skin and tiny, quiet sounds. Her nails dug into my back, her teeth slid over my chin, my neck, my shoulder.

"I want you inside," she whispered into a kiss.

"Not yet."

Although she let out a little growl of frustration, for a while she let me simply kiss her. I loved the way her lips felt on my tongue, the way her tongue felt against my lips. I was acutely aware of every point of contact between us: her breasts against my chest, her hands on my back, the tendons of her thighs pressing into my sides. When she wrapped her legs around mine, her calves felt like a band of heat around me. I reached down and wrapped my hand around the back of her knee, pulling it higher to my hip until I felt my cock slide against her slick skin.

Beneath me, she arched and rocked, getting as much friction as she could without me pushing inside. Kisses would start tentative, maybe playful, and then grow into deep, ravenous, arching hunger before returning to slow and tasting. She let me press her arms over her head, let me suck and bite her nipples almost to the point of pain. She asked me what I wanted, what felt good, and whether I wanted her body or her mouth first. Her first instinct when we were naked was always to pleasure me.

This woman amazed me. I'd lost perspective on who she used to be outside of our relationship. With me, she could be anything. Brave and afraid weren't opposite. She could be sharp and tender, devious and innocent. I wanted to be her everything in the same way.

"I love the way we kiss," she whispered, the words coming out pressed against my lips.

"What do you mean?" I knew what she meant. I knew exactly what she meant; I simply wanted to hear her talk about how fucking perfect it all felt.

"I just love that we kiss the same, that you always seem to know exactly how I want it."

"I want to be married," I blurted. "I want you to marry me."

Fuuuuuuuck.

And so my entire carefully constructed speech was thrown out the window. My grandmother's antique ring was in a box in the dresser—nowhere near me—and my plan to kneel and do everything right just evaporated.

In the circle of my arms, Chloe grew very still. "What did you just say?"

I had completely botched the plan, but it was too late to turn back now.

"I know we have only been together for a little over a year," I explained, quickly. "Maybe it's too soon? I understand if it's too soon. It's just that how you feel about the way we kiss? I feel that way about *everything* we do together. I love it. I love to be inside you, I love working with you, I love watching you work, I love fighting with you, and I love just sitting on the couch and laughing with you. I'm lost when I'm not with you, Chloe. I can't think of anything, or anyone, who is more important to me, every second. And so for me, that means we're already sort of married in my head. I guess I wanted to make it official somehow. Maybe I sound like an idiot?" I looked over at her, feeling my heart try to jackhammer its way up my throat. "I never expected to feel this way about someone."

She stared at me, eyes wide and lips parted as if she couldn't believe what she was hearing. I stood and ran over to the dresser, pulling the box from the drawer and carrying it over to her. When I opened the box and let her see my grandmother's antique diamond and sapphire ring, she clapped a hand over her mouth.

"I want to be married," I said again. Her silence was unnerving, and fuck, I'd completely botched this with my rambling nonsense. "Married to *you*, I mean."

Her eyes filled with tears and she held them, unblinking. "You. Are such. An ass."

Well, that was unexpected. I knew it might be too soon, but an ass? Really? I narrowed my eyes. "A simple 'It's too soon' would have sufficed, Chloe. Jesus. I lay my heart out on the—"

She pushed off the bed and ran over to one of her bags, rummaging through it and pulling out a small blue fabric bag. She carried it back to me with the ribbon hooked over her long index finger, and dangled the bag in my face.

I ask her to marry me and she brings me a souvenir from New York? What the fuck is that? "What the fuck is that?" I asked.

"You tell me, genius."

"Don't get smart with me, Mills. It's a bag. For all I know you have a granola bar, or your tampons, in there."

"It's a ring, dummy. For you."

My heart was pounding so hard and fast I half wondered if this was what a heart attack felt like. "A ring for *me*?"

She pulled a small box out of the bag and showed it to me. It was smooth platinum, with a line of coarse titanium running through the middle.

"You were going to propose to me?" I asked, still completely confused. "Do women even do that?"

She punched me, hard, in the arm. "Yes, you chauvinist. And you totally stole my thunder."

"So, is that a yes?" I asked, my bewilderment deepening. "You'll marry me?"

"You tell me!" she yelled, but she was smiling.

"Technically you haven't asked yet."

"Goddamnit, Bennett! You haven't, either!"

"Will you marry me?" I asked, laughing.

"Will you marry *me*?"

With a growl, I took the box and dropped it on the floor, flipping her onto her back.

"Are you always going to be this impossible?"

She nodded, eyes wide, lip caught between her teeth. *Fuck*. We could settle this later.

"Take my cock." I bent, pressed a kiss into her neck, and groaned when she reached between us to grip me. "Guide it into you."

She shifted her hips beneath me until I could feel myself at her entrance. I slid into her slowly, even though every tendon and muscle in my body wanted it rough and frenzied. I groaned, shivered on top of her, feeling myself sink inside.

Shifting my hips back and then forward, I felt her arms wrap around my neck, her face press into my neck as she rose to meet my movements. It took only two more shifts of my hips before we grew louder and more frantic.

"Give it to me," I whispered into her mouth, licking forward, asking. I lifted her leg, pressed it up to her side and slid in deeper. My eyes rolled closed for a beat and I felt like I was about to explode in her.

She pressed her head back into the pillow, parted her lips to gasp, and I took the opportunity to slide my tongue into her mouth, to suck a little on hers. "That okay?" I whispered, pressing into the skin of her hip with my fingertips. She loved the edge of pain and pleasure, that razor-sharp line we'd discovered early on together. She nodded and I moved faster, filling my head with the smell of her. I tasted her collarbones, her neck, bit a mark into her shoulder.

"Up here," she breathed, pulling me back up to her face. "Kiss me."

So I did. Over and over until she was panting and squirming beneath me, urging me to move faster. I felt her abdomen tense and then her legs squeezed hard around me, her cries sharp in my ear.

Clenching my jaw, I pushed my own release to the back of my mind, wanting more, and longer, and to feel her coming again before I would even let myself drift toward orgasm.

Her cries grew louder, and she screamed and then gasped and tried to pull away but I knew she could come again. I knew she was sensitive but she could take more.

"Don't pull away. You're not done yet. Not even fucking close. Give me another."

Her hips relaxed in my hands; her grip tightened in my hair again.

"Oh." It was just a breath of a sound. There was so much contained in that single, quiet gasp.

I pressed closer, holding her hips and tilting them with my movements. "That's it."

"Coming," she breathed. "I can't—I can't—"

Her hips shook and I gripped her as hard as I dared. "Don't you *fucking* stop."

"Touch me . . . there," she gasped and I knew what she

131

wanted. I kissed her neck before licking my fingers and sliding them to her backside, touching, pressing.

With a sharp cry she came again, the coiled muscles beneath her skin tightening all around my length. Taking a deep breath, I let my orgasm unravel down my back and tear through me; light bursts exploded behind my closed eyes. I could barely hear her hoarse cries over the pounding of blood in my ears.

"Yes yes yes yes . . ." she chanted, delirious, before collapsing onto the pillow beneath her.

It felt like the walls rattled in the silence that followed. Everything in my head shook with need for her; it was disorienting.

"Yes," she gasped one last time.

I held very, very still as awareness seeped back into my thoughts. "Yes?"

Then with her limbs still trembling all around me, and breaths coming out in sharp little pants, she gave me a radiant smile. "Yes . . . I want to be married, too."

Acknowledgments

Thank you to the readers who also wanted more from these two. Your tweets, FB posts, emails, comments, and reviews make us feel like the luckiest chicks out there, and without you, there is no BEAUTIFUL *any-thing*.

Thank you to Adam Wilson for having us howling in laughter while we were editing at midnight on a Tuesday. For two people who claim to be writers, we are surprisingly inarticulate when it comes to expressing how much we value your confidence in us.

Thank you to everyone at Gallery for being game for our silly, smutty words.

Holly Root, thank you for your calm, cool, collected self and for continuing to let us play in every sandbox. And thank you to our families, for being as excited for all of this as we are.

Lo, you put the " ← in my words. Christina, you put the → " in my stories. Race you to the tattoo parlor in Paris.

See how Chloe and Bennett got together in the book that started it all...

"The perfect blend of sex, sass, and heart!"
—S. C. Stephens, bestselling author of *Thoughtless*

Beautiful
BASTARD

A Novel

CHRISTINA LAUREN

I raced down the darkened hall of the now-empty building, the presentation materials clutched haphazardly in my arms, and glanced at my watch. Six twenty. Mr. Ryan was going to have my ass. I was twenty minutes late. As I experienced this morning, he hated late. "Late" was a word not found in the *Bennett Ryan Dickhead Dictionary*. Along with "heart," "kindness," "compassion," "lunch break," or "thank you."

So there I was, running through the empty halls in my stilt-like Italian pumps, racing to the executioner.

Breathe, Chloe. He can smell fear.

As I neared the conference room, I tried to calm my breathing and slowed to a walk. Soft light shone from beneath the closed door. He was definitely in there, waiting for me. Carefully, I attempted to smooth my hair and clothing while tidying the bundle of documents in my arms. Taking a deep breath, I knocked on the door.

"Come in."

I walked into the warmly lit space. The conference room was huge; one wall was filled with floor-to-ceiling windows that gave a beautiful view of the Chicago cityscape from eighteen stories up. Dusk darkened the sky outside, and skyscrapers speckled the horizon with their lighted windows. In the center of the room stood a large heavy wood conference table, and facing me from the head of the table was Mr. Ryan.

He sat there, suit jacket hanging on the chair behind him, tie loosened, crisp white shirtsleeves rolled up to his elbows, and chin resting on his steepled fingers. His eyes were boring into mine, but he said nothing.

"I apologize, Mr. Ryan," I said, my voice wavering with my still labored breathing. "The print job took—" I stopped. Excuses wouldn't help my situation. And besides, I wasn't going to let him blame me for something I had no control over. He could kiss my ass. With my newfound bravery in place, I lifted my chin and walked over to where he sat.

Without meeting his gaze, I sorted through my papers and placed a copy of the presentation on the table before us. "Are you ready for me to begin?"

He didn't respond aloud, his eyes piercing my brave front. This would be a lot easier if he wasn't so gorgeous. Instead, he gestured toward the materials before him, urging me to continue.

I cleared my throat and began my presentation. As I moved through the different aspects of the proposal, he stayed silent, staring directly at his copy. Why was he so calm? His temper tantrums I could handle. But the eerie silence? It was unnerving.

I was leaning over the table, gesturing toward a set of graphs, when it happened.

"Their timeline for the first milestone is a little ambi—" I stopped midsentence, my breath caught in my throat. His hand pressed gently into my lower back before sliding down, settling on the curve of my ass. In the nine months I had worked for him, he had never intentionally touched me.

This was most definitely intentional.

The heat from his hand burned through my skirt and into my skin. Every muscle in my body tensed, and it felt like my insides were liquefying. What the hell was he doing? My brain screamed at me to push his hand off, to tell him to never touch me again, but my body had other ideas. My nipples hardened, and I clenched my jaw in response. *Traitor nipples.*

While my heart pounded in my chest, at least half a minute passed, and neither of us said anything as his hand moved down to my thigh, caressing. Our breathing and the muted noise of the city below were the only sounds in the still air of the conference room.

"Turn around, Miss Mills." His quiet voice broke the silence and I straightened my back, eyes facing forward. Slowly I turned, his hand skimming across me and sliding to my hip. I could feel the way his hand spread from his fingertips on my lower back all the way to where his thumb pressed against the soft skin just in front of my hipbone. I looked down to meet his eyes, which looked intently back at me.

I could see his chest rising and falling, each breath deeper than the last. A muscle twitched in his sharp jaw as his thumb began to move, slowly sliding back and forth, his eyes never leaving mine. He was waiting for me to stop him; there had been plenty of time for me to shove him away, or simply turn and leave. But I had too many feelings to sort out before I could react. I had never felt this way, and I had never expected to feel this about him. I wanted to slap him, and then pull him up by his shirt and lick his neck.

"What are you thinking?" he whispered, eyes somehow both mocking and anxious.

"I'm still trying to figure that out."

With those eyes still locked to mine, he began to slide his hand lower. His fingers ran down my thigh, to the hem of my skirt. He moved it up so his fingertips traced the strap of my garter belt, the lace edge of one thigh-high stocking. A long finger slipped beneath the thin fabric and pulled it down slightly. I sucked in a sharp breath, feeling suddenly like I was melting from the outside in.

How could I let my body react like this? I still wanted to slap him, but now, more than that, I wanted him to keep going. The heavy ache between my legs was building. He reached the edge of my panties and slipped his fingers under the fabric. I felt him slide against my skin and graze my clit before pushing his finger inside me, and I bit my lip trying, unsuccessfully, to stifle my groan. When I looked down at him, beads of sweat were forming on his brow.

"Fuck," he growled quietly. "You're wet." His eyes fell closed and he seemed to be waging the same internal battle I was. I glanced down at his lap and could see him straining against the smooth fabric of his pants. Without opening his eyes, he withdrew his finger and fisted the thin lace of my panties in his hand. He was shaking as he looked up at me, fury clear in his expression. In one quick movement he tore them off, the rip of the fabric echoing in the silence.

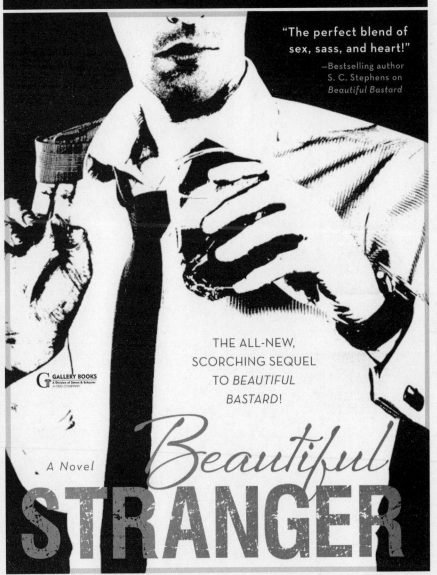

When my old life died, it didn't go quietly. It detonated.

But to be fair, I'd been the one to pull the pin. In just one week I rented out my house, sold my car, and left my philandering boyfriend. And though I'd promised my overprotective parents that I'd be careful, it wasn't until I was actually at the airport that I called ahead to let my best friend know I was moving her way.

That's when it all seemed to sink in, in one perfectly clear moment.

I was ready to start over.

"Chloe? It's me," I said, voice shaking as I looked around the terminal. "I'm coming to New York. I hope the job's still mine."

She screamed, dropped the phone, and reassured someone in the background that she was fine.

"Sara's coming," I heard her explain, and my heart squeezed just thinking about being there with them at the beginning of this new adventure. "She changed her mind, Bennett!"

I heard a sound of celebration, a clap, and he said something I couldn't quite make out.

"What did he say?" I asked.

"He asked if Andy was coming with you."

"No." I paused to fight back the sick feeling creeping up into my throat. I'd been with Andy for six years and no matter how glad I was to be done with him, the dramatic turn in my life still felt surreal. "I left him."

I heard her small, sharp inhale. "You okay?"

"Better than okay." And I was. I don't think I realized exactly *how* okay I was until that moment.

"I think it's the best decision you ever made," she told me and then paused, listening as Bennett spoke in the background. "Bennett says you're going to shoot across the country like a comet."

I bit my lip, holding back a grin. "Not too far off, actually. I'm at the airport."

Chloe screeched some unintelligible sounds and then promised to pick me up at LaGuardia.

I smiled, hung up, and handed the counter attendant my ticket, thinking a comet was too directed, too driven. I was really more like an old star, out of fuel, my own gravity pulling me inward, crushing me. I ran out of energy for my too-perfect life, my too-predictable job, my loveless relationship—exhausted at only twenty-seven. Like a star, my life in Chicago collapsed under the force of its own weight, so I was leaving. Massive stars leave behind black holes. Small stars leave behind white dwarfs. I was barely leaving behind a shadow. All of my light was coming with me.

I was ready to start over as a comet: refuel, reignite, and burn across the sky.

— — —

The club was dark, deafening, and filled with writhing bodies: on the dance floor, in the halls, against the bar. A DJ spun music from a small stage, and flyers plastered all across the front promised that she was the newest and hottest DJ Chelsea had to offer.

Julia and Chloe seemed entirely in their element. I felt like I'd spent most of my childhood and adult life so far at quiet, formal events; here it was as if I'd stepped out of the pages of my quiet Chicago story and into the quintessential New York tale instead.

It was perfect.

I shoved my way up to the bar—cheeks flushed, hair damp, and legs feeling like they hadn't been properly used like this in years.

"Excuse me!" I shouted, trying to get the bartender's attention. Though I had no idea what any of it actually meant, I'd already ordered slippery nipples, cement mixers, and purple hooters. At this point, with the club at maximum density and the music so loud it shook my bones, he wouldn't even look up at me. Admittedly, he was slammed and making such a small number of tedious shots was annoying. But I had an intoxicated, newly affianced friend burning a hole in the dance floor, and said girlfriend wanted more shots.

"Hey!" I called, slapping the bar.

"Sure is doing his best to ignore you, in't he?"

I blinked up—and *up*—at the man pressed close to me at the crowded bar. He was roughly the size of a redwood, and nodded toward the bartender to indicate his meaning. "You never yell at a bartender, Petal. Especially not with what you're going to order: Pete hates making girly drinks."

Of course. It would be just my luck to meet a gorgeous man just days after swearing off men forever. A man with a British accent to boot. The universe was a hilarious bitch.

"How do you know what I was going to order?" My grin grew wider, hopefully matching his, but most likely looking a lot tipsier. I was grateful for the drinks I'd already had, because sober Sara would give him monosyllables and an awkward nod and be done with it. "Maybe I was going to get a pint of Guinness. You never know."

"Unlikely. I've seen you ordering tiny purple drinks all night."

He'd been watching me all night? I couldn't decide if that was fantastic, or a little creepy.

I shifted on my feet and he followed my movements. He had angled features with a sharp jaw and a carved hollow beneath his cheekbones, eyes that seemed backlit and heavy, dark brows, a deep dimple on his left cheek when the grin spread down to his lips. This man had to be well over six feet, with a torso it would take my hands many moons to explore.

Hello, Big Apple.

The bartender returned, then looked at the man beside me expectantly. My beautiful stranger barely raised his voice, but it was so deep it carried without effort: "Three fingers of Macallan's, Pete, and whatever this lady is having. She's been waiting a spell, yeah?" He turned to me, wearing a smile that made something dormant warm deep in my belly. "How many fingers would you like?"

His words exploded in my brain and my veins filled with adrenaline. "What did you just say?"

Innocence. He tried it on, smoothing it over his features. Somehow he made it work, but I could see from the way his eyes narrowed that there wasn't an innocent cell in his body.

"Did you really just offer me three fingers?" I asked.

He laughed, spreading out the biggest hand I'd ever seen on the bar just between us. His fingers were the kind that could curl around a basketball and dwarf it. "Petal, you'd best start with two."

I looked more closely at him. Friendly eyes, standing not too close, but close enough that I knew he had come to this part of the bar specifically to talk to me. "You give good innuendo."

The bartender rapped the bar with his knuckles and

asked for my order. I cleared my throat, steeling myself. "Three blow jobs." I ignored his irritated huff and turned back to my stranger.

"You don't sound like a New Yorker," he said, grin fading slightly but never leaving his constantly smiling eyes.

"Neither do you."

"Touché. Born in Leeds, worked in London, and moved here six years ago."

"Five days," I admitted, pointing to my chest. "From Chicago. The company I used to work for opened an office here and brought me back on to head up Finance."

Whoa, Sara. Too much information. Way to enable stalkers.

It had been so long since I'd even looked at another man. Clearly Andy had been a master in this kind of situation, but unfortunately I had no idea how to flirt anymore. I glanced back to where I expected to see Julia and Chloe dancing, but I couldn't find them in the tangle of bodies on the floor. I was so rusty in this ritual I was practically revirginized.

"Finance? I'm a numbers man myself," he said, and waited until I looked back at him before turning the smile up a few notches. "Nice to see women doing it. Too many grouchy men in trousers having meetings just to hear themselves say the same thing over and over."

Smiling, I said, "I'm grouchy sometimes. I also wear trousers sometimes, too."